Hollywood Psycho:

The Julie Simon Story

Brittany Roth

This book is a work of fiction. Names, businesses, characters, places, incidences, and events are products of the author's imagination. Any resemblance to actual events, places, or persons, living or dead, is coincidental.

Copyright © 2023 Brittany Roth

ISBN: 979-8-9881300-0-0

ISBN (ebook): 979-8-9881300-1-7

www.brittrothauthor.com

Cover design by Sadia Shahid

Interior and formatting by Michael Davie – grimhousepub.com/plans-pricing

To my beautiful Grandmother, my best friend.
I hope I'm making you proud up in heaven.

Dear Reader,

I hope this note finds you well. In this story there are instances that have harassment, sexual assault, rape, abortion and suicide. They do not go into detail. They are said, more so than shown, but are very much alluded to or suggested. I hope that if you do continue to read this story, you enjoy it as it is a very lighthearted thriller that will hopefully leave you satisfied with what you read. And if you need any help please call any of these hotlines for free and anonymous help:

Call or text 988 for the Suicide & Crisis Lifeline or 911 for immediate life-threatening situations.

1(800) 656- HOPE (4673) for the National Sexual Assault Hotline or go to their website www.rainn.org

I hope that you have big dreams, like Julie, and go after them because you are worth every bit of happiness and beauty this life has to offer.

Chapter One

I remember seeing palm trees for the first time. I remember being so mesmerized by their beauty, by their elegance. I know that it sounds ridiculous because it's just a tree, but I feel like they aren't appreciated for what they really are. If you think about it, they are the perfect example of how we should live our lives. What I mean by that is when, for instance, the winds pick up, a palm tree just doesn't fall over. They show us that no matter what tries to bring us down, we can always stand right back up again with our heads held high. Higher than everything that could try to break us; every blow, every gust of wind, every storm that forces us to start losing who we are in this world. But we have that sway within us, for protection, that lets us stand right back up again with even more exuberance and grace than we had before. But, if I'm being honest, what I really love about them is the way the sun hits them when it rises and falls.

Now that's a breathtaking sight! Gosh, I was 21 when I first saw those palm trees. I was so young and so naïve.

I'm 23 now. I guess that that doesn't make me much older, though my mind is definitely in a different place. I wouldn't say that it's darker, it's just not basking in the bright light of innocence anymore.

My parents died in a car accident when I was eight. Since neither of them had any brothers or sisters, I went to live with my grandmother, across town from my childhood home in Arrow Rock, Missouri. She was my best friend, my grandmother, and she encouraged me to be whatever I wanted to be in life—which, at that time, was a famous Hollywood star. My Grandmother loved me so wholeheartedly and with such a passion that I had never seen or experienced before. It wasn't just because I was a kid who suddenly lost her parents and she had to take me in. She genuinely loved me and *wanted* me. We had an inseparable bond and a connection so deep it went further than just a grandmother and her granddaughter. We relied on one another. We trusted each other. And no matter what, I knew that she would always be there for me.

My favorite thing about my grandmother was how we shared a love for the theater and the old greats of the silver screen. That's probably where my love of acting came from, now that I think of it. She could have been a star herself with how beautiful she was. Her auburn eyes always shone so bright, no matter what we were doing. There was always a great light around her, which made people feel a sense of welcome and acceptance; a warmth. She never left the house without getting ready. Sometimes she would say, "Julie remember, life is an event. So you must always be ready." She would smile at me and continue to put on her makeup, which had to be perfect right down to the Pink in the Afternoon Revlon lipstick she always wore. Her favorite movie was Breakfast at Tiffany's, and she would say, "Who wouldn't want to look like Audrey Hepburn?" whenever she caught me staring at her in the mirror before applying some to my own lips. She always wore her hair pulled back with a clip because she said that it accentuated her cheek bones. I always thought it was because it was the only way she knew how to do it. Thinking about it now, she was right. Then there was her signature scent, Charlie Blue. That's a scent I won't ever forget. It's a scent that will always put a smile on my face and make me hear her voice saying, "It makes me feel young."

But, because of her—the way she was and the movies we watched—I grew up admiring Grace Kelly, Maureen O'Hara, Lana Turner, Elizabeth Taylor, and who could forget, Ava Gardner? They were my inspiration growing up in our local community theater. I was kind of a lonely kid. I didn't have very many friends and when I would get invited to birthday parties or sleepovers, I would always wish that I was back at home reading a book or watching a movie with my grandmother. The theater became my outlet for getting through childhood. It was my way to escape reality, by turning into characters that experienced things I knew I may never get the chance to. So, I performed in every play my high school had to offer.

I made it a point to study the greats' every move; from the way they projected their voices, to the way they moved so effortlessly and gracefully across the screen. Even the minute facial expressions they made conveyed so much. Now *that* was acting, and acting was my passion. I wanted to be a famous actress. To be acknowledged alongside one of my idols was my dream. My Grandmother always told me that I should go out into the world and never let anything hold me back. So, that's what I did.

I was almost 20 when she got sick, and I was scared. Who wouldn't be? My Grandmother was the only person that I had in this world. She *was* my world, my everything. How could she leave me?

Watching her slip away from me was the hardest thing that I had ever experienced in my life. When my parents died, yes, I was sad, but it was as if they left in the blink of an eye. Being so young made it easier to move on. But with my grandmother, to whom I had clung to in that time of grief, and who was with me every step of the way, it broke my heart. It was the grief I almost should have felt when my parents died. I kept telling her that I needed her and that I didn't want her to go. She would comfort me the best that she could, until she couldn't anymore. On one of our last days together, she told me to take her money and go out into the world and live my dreams. That would be a dream within itself for anyone, but for me, I would trade whatever money she was talking about to keep her with me a little longer. The very last thing she said to me was, "My sweet Julie, add your name to the list of stars." She died three days later.

After the funeral, and my 21st birthday, I sold the house, packed up my '87 corolla and drove all the way from Missouri to Los Angeles, all by myself, to start my new life. I was alone. I was all that I had in the world. Well, me and my corolla. It wasn't hard letting everything go; all of my memories. I kept some furniture and some mementos, but the rest was my past, and I was now living my future.

It was July 26, 1993; the day that I opened my car door and touched Hollywood soil for the first time. The air was so fresh, and the people were so weird. The first thing to check off of my list was to walk down Hollywood Boulevard to see where I wanted to cement my name, not only with a star, but with my handprints. I found my location right outside Grauman's Chinese Theater, next to Judy Garland. I would somehow get there. I would somehow be a star, in my own right, next to the greats. I was determined.

The first few days, I tried to familiarize myself with this massive, spread out, but beautiful city. I knew that I wanted to live in an area where I would be safe and close to people my own age to hopefully make some friends.

Beverly Hills would be a dream; however, a little out of my price range for the time being. Downtown was too shabby. The Hills would be nice, but Westwood was just right. It was a college town, so there were students all over the place and I would literally be only a few minutes away from Beverly Hills—the place that I would someday call my home. How soon? I wasn't quite sure.

My apartment was on Ashton Avenue and was a one bedroom. Since I only packed what I could fit into my corolla, I didn't have any furniture for about a week, but I had sent for my things that I had put into storage. It was a glorious day when my bed arrived.

Living in my dream land was amazing, but I couldn't help but feel lonely. The only person I had was gone, and although having some of her things with me was comforting, it just wasn't the same. Sure, Los Angeles was busy and fun and full of things to do and see, but when you don't have anyone in your life to share it with, it can be a very lonely place.

My Grandmother had left me $350,000, which was her life savings, plus the money from selling the house. Even though I had enough money to live off of for a few years, I decided to get a job at a restaurant to meet people. And, it was LA—you never knew who you could run into.

I had waitressed back home, in Arrow Rock, at a little diner that most of the locals frequented. Because of my experience, I was able to find a job at a famous, old Holly-wood restaurant, The Musso and Franks Grill, where every other waiter was just like me. We were all trying to break into showbiz.

On my first day, I made friends with a girl named Megan who was from Ohio, and had been in LA for about a year. She had been going on audition after audi-tion—it was impressive. Since I didn't have an agent yet, she said that she would try and set up a meeting for me to meet hers.

"Oh my gosh, he's the best! I go on at least four auditions a week," Megan said with so much excitement in her voice that I couldn't help but reciprocate the same emotion, in the hopes of getting representation. Meeting him would be the jumpstart to my career and the way to get my foot in the door.

"Do I need to bring anything with me? Like a resume or some headshots?" I asked her, eagerly. I wanted to be prepared.

"No, he will set everything up for you if he likes you. And don't worry Julie, he will love you!"

It all seemed to move so fast—too fast—but a week later I was in Dave Clancy's office. Megan had assured me that I would do great and had nothing to worry about, but I just kept thinking that it was a little peculiar that I didn't have to have anything prepared, not even a monologue. As I sat there waiting to see Mr. Clancy, I couldn't help but look around the waiting room, with nerves rattling through me, at all of the headshots on the wall. I didn't recognize anyone. I probably should have taken that as a bad sign, but I had to start somewhere. Maybe Mr. Clancy would be like a first boyfriend—a test run, so to speak.

The receptionist finally called me into his office. As I walked in, my eyes widened with fright when I saw a stout, creepy looking, middle-aged man sitting behind an oversized oak desk, trying to nonchalantly fix the rug he had on his head. When he saw me, he smiled. It wasn't a friendly sight. That crooked, yellow, almost brown smile sent shivers up and down my spine. He was awful to look at. Just awful. Now, even though I had been raised to not judge others, Mr. Clancy was absolutely gross to look at. He had greasy skin that went all the way to the hair that he did have. And his eyes—oh, his eyes—didn't have a lick of kindness behind them. They were dark and ominous, almost black. Just him looking at you made you want to run out of the room, as far away as you could. You shivered like you needed to take a shower and wash his look off of you. It was very uncomfortable. If I wasn't so desperate to become an actress, I would have just turned and walked out. I kept repeating in my head what Megan had told me, that "He was good." So, I figured that I better stick it out and give him the benefit of the doubt, even though everything in me was telling me to run out of the office as fast as I could.

"Julie Simon, is it? Well," he said, as he was biting his lower lip with the yellowest teeth I had ever seen. "You *are* beautiful. Megan tells me that you're new to LA?"

"Yes, I've been here for about a month now," I said, trying to sound as polite as possible. I was finding it hard to not cringe at the sound of his voice.

"What type of training have you had?" he asked.

"Back in Missouri I took theater classes, and I have been in about 20 plays since I was nine. I also took some local acting classes through our community center."

"So, you're theatrically trained, huh?" he said with a look of disgust.

"I guess that's what it would be. There aren't too

many acting opportunities back home, so I kind of took all that I could get."

"Well, I don't know what I can do with you."

"Oh, well I could take some classes out here or I..."

He sat there, staring at me while licking his lips and making a smacking noise that made my stomach churn. "Commercials, I guess," he paused, "Unless," he paused again. "You and I can make an arrangement of some sort?"

"Arrangement?" I asked. "What do you mean by that?" I was caught off guard and was confused, as anyone would be by that sort of question. "What do you mean by *arrangement*?" My heart was now pounding in my throat. I felt as if I was not in the right place, because I most certainly was not.

Dave Clancy got up from behind his desk to reveal his 5'4" stature. He made his way around to me, where he put his hand on my knee and began to move it up, slowly.

My heart was racing, and not in the good way.

"Well, you're a very beautiful woman, Julie, but you're also very forgettable. But I do think that I can do something with you. If you do a little something for me," he winked while running his hand closer and closer to my body.

I began to tense up. I couldn't believe what was happening, but something inside of me made me react. "Get off of me, perv!" I yelled as I pushed him and his hand as far away from me as possible.

"Now, Julie, how do you think this business works?" He cackled. "Do you honestly think that you'll get a movie role just by having a pretty face and being able to mediocrely read a few lines?"

"Well, I'd rather try it that way than have to get felt up by you," I retorted as I rose to leave.

He caught me by the arm and pulled me back. "Julie, let's try to work this out. You give me 30 minutes, and I'll give you a career." He pulled me in closer to him.

I began to edge away, but he kept bringing me in closer and tightly griping my arm until he was kissing my neck. I was in shock from the horror and disgust before me. I was shaking, panicking. I was frozen and didn't know what to do.

There was no way that the entertainment business could really be like this. I had heard stories, but never believed them. And I, Julie Simon, was no casting couch kind of girl. Something inside of me shook me back to reality. With my free hand, I was able to punch him in the gut, which freed my arm and gave me the ability to get out of dodge.

I immediately called Megan as soon as I got home and asked her what the hell she was thinking, sending me to a scumbag like him. And then I asked if she had actually slept with the man to get work.

"Julie, I'm not proud of what I did. But it *is* going to get me somewhere," she said.

"Megan, I can't believe it. I don't want to believe it," I said, still fuming. "It's one thing if he was actually attractive and it had the possibility of going somewhere, but he was absolutely the scum of the earth and is *not* going to get you *any* acting jobs, anywhere." I hated myself for hurting her feelings, but she was the closest person to me at this point in my life, and I wanted her to succeed. My Grandmother would have said it to me, so I said it to her.

"Well, we'll see," was all she said, in a hateful tone, before hanging up.

Thoughts of whether tinsel town was really like this kept pouring through my brain. Back home, people were always so polite and wouldn't do things that went against their morals to get ahead in life. I was flabbergasted with what someone so young and so stupid would do, just for a chance at a possible audition, with no guarantee of actually getting casted and securing a future.

Megan avoided me at work from then on. She went as far as changing every shift that she had with me. I ended up making friends with some of the guys that worked there, Jeffery and Dawson. There was no attraction there; they were both absolutely gorgeous, and gay. Which was a bummer, but it was actually kind of better; I had two guys who made me feel safe and protected. Jeffery and Dawson took me around the city and showed me where all of the celebrities liked to hangout, and where *we* needed to hangout if we wanted to get discovered.

Jeffery was a model and had been in a few watch campaigns. He was 6'1" with the perfect California tan, light brown, almost blonde, hair, killer blue eyes, and muscles you could tell he went to the gym for. He was the quintessential "California Boy." Dawson, on the other hand, was a struggling theatrical actor, like myself, trying to get on the silver screen. He was too gorgeous to pass up, though. Dawson was 5'10" 'On a good day,' as he would say. He had dark brown hair, dark brown eyes, a California tan, and abs for days. His jawline could cut like a knife. He also had the most perfect teeth, which made for the most perfect smile. He had been in a tooth-paste commercial and a condom commercial. He didn't have any lines in either; he was strictly in them for his stunning good looks and jealousy worthy bone structure.

"Julie, you are too cute! If I was straight, I would snatch you up in a second," Dawson would always say to me.

"Not if I got hitched to her first," Jeffery would chime in.

"Guys, guys, it's okay, we could be swingers! Or, Dawson could be my weekday husband and Jeffery, you could be my weekend husband," I would joke back.

"I get her longer!" Dawson would say, while kissing me on the cheek.

"But I get to have all of the fun!" Jeffery would counter back, with a wink.

The boys made me feel like I had family. They loved coming over and hanging out. We would talk about our dream roles over a glass of wine, or spend evenings laughing at what some of our co-workers had said about customers. We grew close, and I didn't feel so alone knowing that one of them would always be there for me. They loved my small-town ambitions of making it big in the city, but I didn't want to reveal too much about myself. I didn't want them to think that I was some sort of hanger-oner. I told them that my parents still lived back in Missouri, and that I was planning on visiting them in a few weeks. I guess that I just didn't want people to feel sorry for me or to take pity on the little orphan girl. I had that growing up in a small town, and I hated the feeling of being felt sorry for. I wanted a fresh start, so I took this as my opportunity to make it happen.

One night, the three of us went out to celebrate Jeffery's new underwear campaign. I had quickly downed a few drinks and got to talking to this handsome stranger, who just so happened to be an agent.

"I can tell that you really want this," he said.

"I really do," I said back, confidently.

"Why don't you prepare a monologue and come by my office? I'll see if you have what it takes," he winked. "I would do it here, but I think that we need a more appropriate setting," he smiled.

I was apprehensive because of my last encounter with a so called 'Hollywood Agent,' and I think that he could tell.

"I promise that I won't bite. My partner and I are always looking for new talent, and I know that she'll love you."

A 'she!' There was a 'she' that would be there. "Yeah, I'll see you Monday," I smiled, much more at ease.

My LA luck must have turned around, because on Monday I was in his office and auditioned in front of not only him, but his partner, Anita Jones. I had heard from word of mouth that Anita Jones was the agent that you wanted to jumpstart your career. And here, by fate or by my grandmother's influence, I was standing in front of her, reciting my 9th grade monologue from a play called

'Go Home Charlie,' which my teacher had actually written.

"Charlie, I told you that I never wanted to see your sad, silly little face anymore. We never had anything real. All it was, was puppy love. You knew that we were never really going anywhere, right? You had to have known that I would move on from you. Charlie, please. Just go home, Charlie, I don't want you anymore. Just leave. Leave me alone. Home, Charlie, go home."

Okay, so it wasn't the best monologue, but out of the catalogue of monologues that I had stored in my brain, that was the first one to pop out. It's all in the delivery, and deliver I did!

They seemed impressed. I was shaking on the inside, all while trying to contain my outer composure. Right then and there, Anita Jones *herself* told me that she would like to represent me.

"You're unique," she said. "You have this naïve innocence about you. It must be that whole small town vibe thing. I'd like to represent you, Julie."

It was definitely my grandmother. She was looking down on me. She was the one who made this happen.

Chapter Two

In early August, I went on my very first audition for a fast-food commercial. Auditioning has got to be one of the scariest things to ever do. I mean, you're just standing there, alone, in front of a handful of people who are judging you. They are literally just sitting there, watching you, and deciding whether or not you are good enough. Like, actually *good enough* to make people believe that you are this made-up person. It's nerve-wracking, yet thrilling.

"Take your mark," the casting director said. "Action."

"Now with a tasty, toasted bun—"

"Cut. Thank you, next," he said. That fast and that emotionless.

I didn't get that one. I didn't even get a callback.

Dawson had me start taking an acting class with him to help us try and break the theatrical mold and sculpt our crafts into ones ready for film. I tried to take in all that I could, but acting was starting to become more difficult. I wasn't comfortable doing intimate scenes with guys from our class. One time, two other students were performing together and the guy got *aroused*. I had to look away. Everyone thought that the scene was great, but I just felt embarrassed and self-conscious. Another thing that made it difficult was that in every class and every audition, there were always at least ten, almost identical, copies of me: brown hair, green eyes, pale skin, slim build. How was I supposed to stick out amongst *myself*? But I kept persevering, and one day, I got a call from Anita Jones.

Somehow, Anita waved her magical wand over her rolodex and got me an audition with the biggest director in the industry, Richard Harrington. This was a major deal. If you were cast in a Richard Harrington film, the window of opportunities would be endless. This audition would be *the* audition. The one that could either make my career, or break it.

I remember arriving early so that I could run my lines and try to get rid of my nerves. As I sat in the corner, a beautiful blonde captured my attention. She captured everyone's attention, and she wasn't afraid to have it on her. My eyes could only look at her as she walked past everyone as if she was the only one in the room. I've always wanted to be able to do that.

The way she walked, or moreso glided, down the hallway was intimidating. She had this air of elegance about her. I couldn't help noticing how she held her shoulders pulled back, with her head held high, and she would give the slightest head tilt when she acknowledged someone.

She had a jaw dropping smile, with the most perfect, gleaming, blonde hair that glistened when the light hit it just right, leaving anyone in her wake envious. I had never seen someone have so much confidence and arrogance at the same time. My eyes could barely come off of her, that's how beautiful she was. I could feel my cheeks starting to blush, but I couldn't help but follow her with my gaze, down the hallway and disappearing through the doors that soon would be calling out my name. The part was definitely going to her.

Just as my nerves were growing intensely from the self-shattering ego of this stranger, "Julie Simon?" the assistant said. "You're up." My heart sank.

The tension in that room, I can't even begin to describe. It was almost unbearable. My breathing quickened, and my heart began beating all the way up in my throat. I had never felt more pressure and fear from nerves than what I was feeling at that moment. But this was it. This was my chance to make something of myself.

"Julie Simon?" a snarky woman in glasses asked.

"Yes," I said with a smile. I still can't fathom how I was able to get that out.

"Originally from Missouri?" she snarked again.

"Yes," was the only reply I could come up with. My mind was blank.

I scanned my eyes slightly to the right and saw Richard Harrington sitting there, just a few feet away from me. How could I have not noticed him before? Maybe because he was just sitting there, not looking at me or acknowledging me in any way. That made me freak out even more. Then my mind started to race. Why *wasn't* he paying any attention to me? Was it what I was wearing? Jeans and a tee shirt? My brunette hair? The way I looked? I know that I wasn't as beautiful as the girl before me, but I knew that I deserved a chance.

"You may begin when you're ready," Mr. Harrington finally said, without looking up.

Slate. Remember to slate. *Breathe.* Remember to breathe. Here it was, my make-or-break moment.

"Hi! My name is Julie Simon and I am 21 years old." I paused, took a deep breath, and began.

"Danny, I told you already. I need space."

"Why, Rachel? Why don't you love me anymore?" The assistant read in the driest way possible, making it harder to get a feel for the scene.

"I just moved on is all. Did you really expect me to stray?" My eyes widened and I froze. I messed up my line. "I mean, stay?"

My face was burning at this point. I lost the role with that foul up. I just knew it. There was a slight pause from all. Everyone's eyes turned toward Richard Harrington, who still appeared to be interested in whatever he was looking at. But he gave the hand motion to continue.

"Rachel, I love you and I know that we can make this

work," the assistant read, even more blandly, as if she already knew the audition was over.

Panic came over me as I flustered for my line, so I improvised. "Well, Danny, this just isn't working anymore. We can't be together. Here's, it's... it's not you, it's me..."

"Cut," Mr. Harrington yelled, unimpressed. "Bye."

I blew my big chance. My heart had never felt failure and sadness quite like this, and my heart had handled a lot. Tears began to run down my cheeks as I walked out of the door. I closed my eyes and leaned against the hallway wall, trying to hold in my cries of anger for myself. I couldn't hold them in, though, and I sank to the floor.

"You did a good job," a strange voice said.

"No, I did horrible," I groaned. "I'm never going to make it here. I should just go back home," I said with my face buried in my hands.

"Don't get so down on yourself, you'll probably get the next one."

"Thanks," I replied, wiping my tears. As I slowly looked up, I was surprised to see that the blonde beauty was the one reassuring me. Something then came over me. "That was my first big audition, I'm not even sure how I really got it." I smirked. My heart started pounding. "I blew it."

"It couldn't have been that bad, trust me," she smiled. "So, where are you from?"

"Missouri. I've been here for about three months now. I'm starting to think that coming here was a mistake, though."

Without hesitation, she exclaimed, "Come on! I'm taking you to lunch and I won't take no for an answer." She grabbed my arm and began to pull me down the hall.

"Wait. Aren't you going to audition?"

"No. I was just here to see my father, but that can wait until later." Her confidence exuded.

She kept pulling me down the hallway, which led to her pulling me down a staircase.

"I'm Julie," I semi-yelled. "Julie Simon."

"I'm Roxanne Harrington, but everyone calls me Roxy." She winked at me with that million-dollar smile.

I could feel my eyes growing with shock. The daughter of Richard Harrington, legendary director, was taking *me* to lunch? I had just cried in front of her, basically making a fool of myself. What if she told her father? He would *never* want me in any project—ever. What was I doing? Composure. I needed to keep my composure.

"Where are we going?" I asked, coolly.

"This great little diner, not too far from here," Roxy responded.

We got outside and began walking towards the parking lot, Roxy still pulling me along like a dog.

"Oh, by the way, I'm calling you Jules," she turned and said back to me, before proceeding to pull me to her white Mercedes. "Is it okay if I put the top down?"

"Yeah, definitely!" I smiled, holding back my excitement.

Roxy was being so nice to me, which she didn't have to be, seeing as we were strangers, but I wanted her to be my friend. I needed her to be my friend. I had Jeffery and

Dawson, but I needed a friend who was a girl. Someone to relate to, or tell personal things to; everyone needs that. Maybe this beautiful, 5'9" blonde with the most beautiful chestnut brown eyes would be my new friend. My new "Hollywood" Best Friend!

A short drive later, we pulled up to the Hollywood Hills Coffee Shop. The 1960's style décor reminded me of the diner I worked at back home in Arrow Rock. It kind of made me feel like I was home. I followed Roxy to the back corner where we were approaching a booth with three guys in it.

"Hey guys, this is Jules. She's my new friend so be nice, okay?" She said it with authority. But most importantly, she called me her *friend*. "Jules, this is Chad..."

"Hi," Chad said.

"Sebastian..." Roxy continued.

"Sup?" Sebastian waved.

"And Dalton," she ended.

"Hello." The simple word came out of his mouth in the smoothest, drawing-you-in kind of way, while nodding his head ever so slightly and looking me directly in my eyes. Who was this mysterious guy, and why did I have this instant urge to want to know everything about him?

"Hello," I shyly said back, without being able to take my eyes off of the most ruggedly sexy man I had ever laid my eyes on. My whole body was tingling with wonder for him. It was like I already knew him and had to have him be mine. He just had this mysterious aura around him that I had to figure out.

That day—that first encounter, that first hello—will always be in my mind as one of the greatest days of my life. I mean, I met Chad and Sebastian, but they were your typical Beverly Hills rich kids. Dalton, on the other hand, was unlike anyone I had ever met or seen before.

Chad Remington had good looks and knew it. His uniform was brightly colored polo shirts, khakis, and deck shoes, to be ready to take a girl sailing at a moment's notice. His father owns Remington Financial, which is a multi-billion-dollar consulting company. He caters to celebrities and other wealthy people. But Chad wasn't, let's just say, as smart as his father. Chad grew up with a staff of 30 in his household at all times. He never had to lift a finger for anything and was used to getting everything that he wanted, and I mean *everything*.

That day at the diner, he was so excited because his dad had just bought him a new BMW 321i convertible. And let me tell you, that car! I laugh about it now, but we had some pretty terrifying experiences with him behind the wheel. He was sweet, though. I remember one time he randomly stopped by my apartment with Sebastian because they were in the neighborhood and wanted to say hi. He was kind of like a big, goofy brother. He was all about girls, but he had a big heart. At least, that's how he appeared to me.

Then we have Sebastian Porter, or as I like to refer to him, Chad's sidekick. He was strikingly handsome, but so loud and obnoxious that his personality alone turns you off from him. His mother was an actress and his father was a producer, who occasionally worked with Roxy's Dad. Sebastian was raised by nannies, so he was used to getting his way as well. His parents bought him their love, and his nannies were too afraid to lose their jobs, so they always said yes to him. I think that being neglected by his parents definitely made him the way that he was—the guy who is always trying to be the center of attention and needing approval. That's why he's the loud guy at the party, but he still needs to be guided. That's where his sidekick nature comes in. He would crack some hilarious jokes though, which made him a little more endearing.

And then there's Dalton. How could I ever forget him? Let me tell you about Dalton Blake. First of all, he was the most gorgeous guy I had ever seen. He had leading man movie star looks. The tall, dark and handsome type. He was that bad boy that made every girl's heart skip a beat. The one that no matter how hard you try, you can't stop thinking—or fantasizing—about him. He's the kind of guy that every time you close your eyes at night, you see his face and pretend that he's the pillow you are squeezing so tight. He had the sexiest hair that he would slick back in a cool, effortless way. Kind of like he wasn't trying, and didn't care how it turned out; but it was always perfect. He was like a modern-day James Dean, with piercing, green eyes that you could feel undressing you; like he was memorizing every inch and curve of your body. The way that he smiled that perfect crooked smile at you sent the good kind of tingling to all of the right places. And when he would lick his supple, irresistible lips, you couldn't help but imagine them kissing you all over your lust-ridden body.

There isn't a day that goes by that I don't think about him. He's *that* kind of guy. The one that you can't live without. The one that you fantasize about all day long. The one that you pray wants you. The kind of guy that you'd do anything for. He's *that* guy. The guy that you live and breathe for. He is the air that fills your lungs, the bones that keep you together, the skin that protects you and the sleep that you need so that you can see him in your dreams. He's the guy that always stays with you, no matter what happens; he'll always be on your mind.

Dr. Blake, Dalton's father, was a plastic surgeon to the stars and a restaurant investor. His mom, Mrs. Blake, had been a stay-at-home Mom since she married Dalton's father, but she was once a groupie for all of those cool rock bands in the 60's.

Dalton was a ladies' man; much like his father, who sleeps with his patients. Let's just say that he's *known* around town.

When Dalton was 16, he moved into his own Beverly Hills mansion at the request of his mother, who said that he was "ready to leave home." Can you imagine what that would be like? You could do anything. But Dalton was the quiet, mysterious bad boy. Is there any other kind? He had everything growing up; even a chauffeur on call if he didn't feel like driving his 1970 Chevelle. See? Even his car was sexy. He grew up similar to Chad and Sebastian, yet he carried himself as someone wiser beyond their years. That's what drew you into him. Although he had this bad boy persona, there seemed to be more to him underneath the surface, and that's what made him unforgettable.

His voice! Oh, his voice! Soft yet rugged, raspy, yet so easy to listen to. Even a little clear of his throat made your whole body completely lust for him. I fell madly in love with him the second I saw him, and I still am. Even to this day.

Dalton Blake.

Roxy sat next to Chad, which left an opening next to Dalton. My heart had never raced so rapidly in my life. My palms were sweating, my face felt like it was on fire, and it took everything in me to not go into convulsions from my nerves.

"Rox, you missed it. There was some major eye candy that passed by before you walked in," Sebastian said.

"Yeah, and Sebastian *thinks* that he could have banged her," Chad chimed in.

"No, I totally could have, and I *would* have if Rox didn't come up," Sebastian argued.

"Dude, she was long gone before the girls walked up," Chad said, making it seem as if I were one of them.

Was I dreaming? I already felt like I was one of them, like I was a lifelong friend. I mean, how were these "Beverly Hills" kids so nice and accepting? I was a nobody from Missouri. Didn't they have a reputation to uphold?

Why were they being so nice? Especially to me. I guess my perception of them being snobby was way off, because they seemed far different than what you see in the movies.

"So, Jules, what part of the world do you come from?" Chad asked me.

"I'm from Missouri," I replied.

"More like misery," Sebastian butted in.

"Come on, Seb," Roxy said as she glared at him.

"Diss!" Chad joked. "So how long have you been living in beautiful Hollywoodland?"

I was so nervous. I felt like I was being interrogated, but if I wanted to fit in with the 'cool kids' I had to *be* one. I'm an actress, it should have been easy. "About three months now," I said with a smile.

"Rad," Sebastian paused. "Bro, I could have totally nailed that girl."

"Yeah, right," Chad responded.

My face must have been making a weird expression, because Roxy was looking at Dalton with her own expression that I can't even describe. I was still so immersed by the seductive nature that Dalton was giving off that I couldn't even move my eyes over to see his reciprocating look. I was almost paralyzed with nerves.

"The things that I would do to her—" Chad began saying before Roxy interrupted.

"The things that *I* would do to her..." she paused with a far-off, sensual look on her face. "I would have definitely banged her."

"Keep going," Sebastian encouraged.

"Yes! Please!" Chad added.

"A lady never tells, boys. I didn't even see the broad and I know that I would have been able to get her in the sack over you, Sebastian," she said, reaching for his soda.

Chad started laughing and agreeing. I was a little uncomfortable with the conversation, aside from being among extremely attractive strangers, so I got up and walked away. I didn't want to leave, because Roxy was my ride back to my car, so I decided to go to the restroom to get myself together.

Just then, I felt a hand on my shoulder. "Hey Jules," the smoldering voice said.

My face lit up as I slowly turned around to face, head on, the irresistible Dalton Blake.

"Hey, I'm sorry about them. They're kind of morons. They don't really know how to act in front of a lady." He was perfect, and knew just what to say.

"It's okay," I replied, shyly.

"So, three months huh? How're we treating you?" he asked.

Let's see, *I haven't been able to make a lot of friends, I am completely lonely and missing my grandmother and wish that she was still alive and with me. I was sexually harassed by a disgusting agent who wanted me on the casting couch. I just blew a major audition that could have been my big break, and now I am completely in love with you. So, it's been great!*

I couldn't tell if this was just him, or if he was possibly interested in me. The natural shyness quality in me was in full force.

"It's been okay. I found an apartment in Westwood so—"

"Westwood! That's not too far from where I am," Dalton interrupted.

"Yeah, it's nice there! I also work at the Musso and Franks Grill, and," I paused. "I'm an actress," I continued.

"An actress, huh?"

"Yeah, I was actually just at an audition when I met Roxy."

"So, what have you been doing for fun since you've been here?" He changed the subject.

"Umm, nothing really. I've gone out to a few bars with some friends from work, but that's pretty much it. I kind of stick to myself. I read a lot," I shrugged.

Dalton then put his perfectly muscular, leather jacket wearing arm around me and said, "Well, maybe you and I can get together, and I can *really* show you what this town is like."

My heart. It was racing, and I was blushing. Maybe my grandmother was making this happen too.

"I'd really like that," I replied.

He just smiled. "I'll see you back at the table."

I smiled back and went into the restroom, trying to contain the squeals welling up inside of me.

When I got back, I was feeling more like myself again but with an added quality that I never had before. I was now *cool*. I'd never felt that way before. It felt good.

As I sat down next to Dalton, Roxy handed me a napkin that she had written her phone number and address on in red lipstick. "Here, so we can hangout more often."

I smiled and reached inside my purse for a pen and wrote my information for her. "Here's mine."

"Awesome," she smiled. "I'm so glad I met you, Jules. I have such a good feeling about you. You're way cooler than these dorks," she nudged at Chad.

"Yeah, me too. You guys all seem really cool." I instantly felt lame for saying that.

"We need to do something fun this weekend," Sebastian interrupted. "I'm so bored of doing the same thing."

"Well, what did you have in mind, Sebastian?" Roxy asked, seeming annoyed.

"I don't know."

Roxy sighed heavily, rolling her eyes.

"Let's just hang out at Dalton's," Chad shrugged.

"That's the bored I was talking about. We always do that."

Dalton let out a little cough and outstretched his arms across the top of the booth. I looked towards him and shyly smiled, feeling the blood rush to my cheeks. He looked at me and smiled back while lightly brushing his fingertips over my shoulder.

Maybe, *finally*, LA was coming around. Maybe it was finally going to let me have a little bit of good luck; first, by becoming friends with the right people, and then, maybe falling in love.

Chapter Three

By the time I got home from the diner, I was so excited to be part of an actual friend group that I didn't even know what to do with myself. I couldn't help thinking that I wasn't Julie from Missouri anymore; I was Jules from Westwood. By some blessing from above—I'm thinking my grandmother—my life was becoming everything I ever wanted it to be: glamorous. I was living in the right place, working on my career, and now I was in with the right people.

My phone began ringing when I got out of the shower. When I answered it, I almost dropped my towel.

"Jules, it's Roxy."

"Hey, Roxy! I had so much fun today! Thanks for—" I began, but she quickly cut me off.

"I was thinking. We should have a girl's night. Do you want to come over and hangout? We'll have some girl talk, have some margaritas, make a night out of it?" Roxy asked.

"Umm," I paused, excited that she had invited me over, but I had just met this girl. Should I be staying over at her house already? I didn't truly know who she was or who she could be. I just knew that she was my friend. "Yeah, I'd love to!"

"Great! I'll see you soon then!" She hung up.

My heart was racing, but it was the kind of racing that happens for something good and exciting. You know, the kind of excited that you get the night before the first day of school, or the kind of excited you get before a first date. I packed an overnight bag and was on my way.

It wasn't a very long drive to get to Roxy's house, but as I drove past all of the gorgeous homes, I was thinking about Dalton. The more I thought of him, the more I couldn't wait for the time when he would 'show me around town.' The anticipation of being alone with him, just the two of us, put a giddy kind of smile on my face and butterflies in my stomach. I felt like I was in high school again, having a crush on the most popular guy in school. But it made me really happy, and I hadn't truly felt that way in a while.

Then I noticed something that took my attention away from Dalton. Every street I passed was lined with a different type of tree. I thought that was interesting, and my curious brain wondered why. But then a sense of fullness took over my heart as I turned onto Roxy's palm tree lined street and a smile returned to my face. God, those palm trees were beautiful. I know it sounds stupid, because it's a palm tree—basically, a gigantic piece of grass—but they just stood there, watching over everything. They fascinated me. They give off this cool California vibe that you can't get anywhere else. Yeah, they have them in other places but there's nothing like looking at one with a California sunset as its backdrop. That's when you feel like anything could happen.

I finally pulled up to a French style mansion that I can only describe as absolutely breath-taking. My little '87 Corolla definitely looked out of place next to the Rolls Royce in the driveway and Roxy's little Mercedes. In that instant, all of my fantasies about being famous one day went out the window, and I went back to being Julie from Missouri.

A housekeeper greeted me at the door and called out for Roxy. My only thought was, *I hope her dad isn't here.* I wouldn't even know what to do with myself if he remembered me—not that he would—but I'd probably just run out the door to my car and drive home. Or hide under a rock somewhere. They were both good options at the time.

Roxy came gliding down the stairs, like Rita Hayworth in 'Cover Girl', descending the spiral ramp in a sheer, fur-lined robe, with her beautiful blonde hair perfectly floating behind her. It was a scene straight out of a movie, playing right before my own eyes. You could almost hear the orchestra playing and somehow, the room filled with light. I was almost starstruck.

"You're finally here!" she said as she hugged me. "Rosie, bring Jules' bag to my room," she said, grabbing my arm and proceeding to give me a tour.

"Not so Missouri, huh?" she said with a wink.

I shook my head.

"Welcome to Beverly Hills! You'll get used to it, especially hanging out with me!" I couldn't tell if she was trying to brag or trying to encourage me as a new friend in some strange way. That's the thing about Roxy Harrington; you could never tell what her real intentions were. Let me put it this way, if life was a poker game, she had the best face.

We proceeded on a tour through the most extravagant home I had ever been in. There was a library, a game room, and even a movie viewing room—but that one made sense. It all seemed so surreal; to be here, surrounded by all of these things that felt unattainable at one point in my life. But there I was, looking around, taking it all in, and telling myself that one day I would have a house exactly like this: perfect, elegant and classy, just like my old Hollywood starlets. Although it was beautiful and captured my attention from the moment I stepped foot inside, I had never seen a home look so unlived in. It felt a little cold; like you couldn't touch anything because everything had a specific place. It was more of a museum than a home. So, I made a mental note that even though I wanted this, I wanted it to feel cozy and lived in. Like an actual home, not just a house.

Roxy was like a dream as she paraded me around,

showing me this and that. This girl had everything, wanted for nothing, and could get anything that she wanted. She had an exuberance about her, and it was captivating. She just kept drawing you in.

Her bedroom. God, her bedroom was bigger than my apartment. It looked like a palace, with gold-trimmed detail on the walls and furniture. Everything was so elegant. The tub in her bathroom looked more like a swimming pool than just a place to relax and get clean. And her closet! Her closet was basically Fred Segal right there in her own home. It was huge. I had to clench my teeth together to keep my jaw off of the floor.

"How poster boy is Dalton?" Roxy asked, jumping onto her king-sized bed.

"Yeah, he's okay." I didn't want Roxy to know that I was already madly in love with Dalton, so I answered as normal as possible.

"Okay?" she questioned. "Dalton Blake is *not* just okay, he's babelicious!"

She had me there. There was absolutely *no way* to disagree with her. Dalton *was* incredibly good looking. I couldn't help but think of him, and I smiled at Roxy, blushing.

Roxy began flipping through magazines, commenting on all of the models and their designer outfits. She told me what she already had, what was in the process of being shipped, and what she was going to get. Her life seemed so fabulous; like it was straight out of a movie. One day, my life would be like that. My life would be a movie. And I would have everything I ever wanted.

Music had already been playing when we arrived in her bedroom, and when "Good Vibrations" came on, Roxy couldn't help but gloat about how she had slept with Marky Mark. Then she quickly went back to Dalton. "So, back to Dalton. What do you *really* think about him?"

My heart began to race. "Why?" I asked.

"Oh, I'm just curious," she said.

Oh boy! That was a loaded question. I mean, what could I say about Dalton Blake without professing my love for him after only just meeting him that afternoon? "He's nice. He's handsome," I paused. "It's probably the same way that you feel about him," I answered, hoping that she would drop the conversation.

"Definitely NOT! I only date older men. Dalton's cute and all, but he doesn't have the experience of an older man, or the ruggedness," she passionately said. "But when I do need a fix, Chad and Sebastian are my go-to to get my rocks off."

I'm a pretty small-town girl. Hearing that when Roxy needed to have sex that she would just go out and have it —or even that she was having sex at all—was unreal to me. My Grandmother had raised me with values and morals, and Roxy didn't seem to have any. I know that we grew up in different states and at different paces, but I was kind of put off by her loose behavior. It was like she didn't respect herself. But I wanted to be Roxy's friend, so I smiled and played it off as if I knew what she was talking about. I mean, I'm an actress, right?

Some time passed while we continued to flip through magazines and listen to music. We were continuing to get to know one another when Roxy jumped up, faster than a cat that spotted a snake, and practically scared me to death.

"I have an idea!" she exclaimed. "I am *exhausted* from being the only girl in our little group, and well, I know that the guys liked you. So, you should be our new member!"

"Really!?" I was so excited. I felt like I was in high school again, but in an alternate reality. In that moment, I silently thanked my grandmother; it was her making this happen.

"Yes, really! Or else I wouldn't have asked you, Jules. You are so funny!" she said. "Oh, and don't worry, I won't tell Dalton about how red in the face you get whenever I mention his name." She winked as she walked into her closet.

It was a night of getting to know each other. Just two strangers, bonding over little things that connected our two very different worlds. She became more than a friend. She became someone I looked up to. Someone I could tell things to. Confide in. Someone I could trust.

"I'm an only child," I told her after she asked about my family in Missouri.

"No way! Me too!"

"Really?"

"Yeah, did you love it or what?" she asked.

I shrugged. "I guess it was okay. I mean, all of the focus was on me. It would have been nice to have a brother or sister to talk to or hang out with sometimes." I paused. "I was kind of a loner back home. I just didn't really fit in with the people there. And the boyfriends I had never lasted more than a few weeks."

Roxy grabbed my hand and began to squeeze it. "Well, you fit in now. Moving here was probably the best thing you could've ever done."

I smiled.

"I don't think things happen coincidentally. I think they happen for a reason. You were supposed to move here because you were meant to meet me."

"I think you're right!"

"Oh, I'm always right," she smiled, that confidence and arrogance emitting from her. Then she started to sniff her nose before excusing herself to the restroom. "I'll be right back. I have to use the powder room."

"Okay." I sat there on her bed, happy that I now had such a great friend. As I looked around her room, I couldn't help but think, *How could life get any better than this?*

Moments later, she walked back out, still sniffling but now wiping her nose. "Are you okay?" I asked.

"Yeah, it's just my allergies. I've told Rosie to not let my mom's dog in my room, but sometimes she still let's that little bastard in here," she said, sitting back down on her bed. "I'll be okay. I'm used to it."

The following day, Roxy and I had breakfast out by her pool. After we ate, she said that she had to go to an appointment, so I left. I got home and watched a little bit of MTV before I had to get ready for work.

Jeffery and Dawson ambushed me immediately, wanting to know how my audition went with Richard Harrington.

"Did you get the part?" Dawson asked.

"No," I answered.

"Well, did he seem interested? What was he like? Was he gorgeous?" Jeffery asked.

"He is very intimidating. Handsome, yes. But I could barely hold myself back from running out of the room." I paused and casually continued, "I did, however, meet his daughter Roxy. Well, actually, she came up to—"

"Wait, you met Roxy Harrington?" Dawson asked.

"I saw her on Rodeo once. She was such a bitch, but absolutely stunning," Jeffery said.

"Yeah, she is beautiful, but she's actually really, really nice. She came up to me when she saw me crying after the audition and took me to lunch," I said.

"No way!" Dawson's eyes widened. "You went to lunch with her? What was she like?" he eagerly asked.

"She's really sweet. We met three of her guy friends there, Chad, Sebastian and Dalton Blake," I said, trying to hold back my smile, although I could feel my cheeks heating up.

"Oh my God, I've seen those guys before out at some

bars on Sunset. They're *really* good looking, especially that Dalton guy," Jeffery said.

"Yeah, they're cool too. We just had some lunch and then when I got home, Roxy called me and asked me to stay the night at her house for a girl's night. So, I went last night." I shrugged coolly.

"Are you serious?" Jeffery asked.

"Yes," I answered back.

"So, you stayed the night in the house of *the most famous* movie director in the world last night?" Dawson paused, baffled. "Did you see him? Was he there? Did he remember you?" he rambled on.

"Yes, no, no, and I don't know if he would. His head was down basically the entire audition. Which is probably good, seeing that I am friends with his daughter now."

"Friends?" Dawson questioned.

"Yeah, she asked me if I wanted to be a part of their group," I said, smiling.

"That is *so* cool," Jeffery said.

"Well, just don't forget about us little people when you are gallivanting around Beverly Hills," Dawson quipped with a snooty accent.

"How could I? You guys are my best friends here." I said it with a smile.

"No, but really, just be careful Julie. I know that they're beautiful and flashy..."

"Yeah, and extremely rich," Dawson interrupted.

"Right. But just don't let them get to your head and forget about us, because we love you," Jeffrey said with sincerity in his voice.

"I won't. I promise." But I still felt guilty that I was more excited about my *new* friends than I was about them.

Chapter Four

A few days went by without any word from Roxy. Not hearing from her was all that I could think about. It became my obsession. I know that I had just met her, but I couldn't help wondering if I had done something to make her not like me. Or was it Chad or Sebastian that didn't like me? I may have made a face or two in response to their conversation at the diner, but nothing noticeable. Or maybe it was Dalton. He *had* offered to show me around, but he was probably just trying to be nice. God, I hoped that it wasn't him. I couldn't continue living if he didn't like me. Having a thing for Dalton Blake was kind of like having a celebrity crush right within reach. It was the rush of not knowing if he wanted you back that kept you wanting him more. And the more I thought about him, the more intense my feelings for him grew. And that was after only meeting him once. It was like I knew him without actually knowing him, which made it all the more nerve-wracking just waiting around to hear from them. All in all, I think I was just hoping that Roxy didn't hate me. I played it pretty cool when we hung out, and I knew that I wasn't really "one of them," but Roxy made it seem like I could be. She did ask me if I wanted to join them, to be one of them. But what did that even really mean, to be "one of them?" A friend? An acquaintance? A companion? What? That's what made me want to be closer to them. The allure that they had around all of them was exhilarating.

I just felt like a fool. Why would these perfect, young, elite class people want anything to do with me? They grew up having everything, and the only everything that I ever had was no longer with me. It just seemed like it could have been the greatest thing in the world; to have these friends that the people back home never really thought existed. The type of friends that were beautiful and didn't care what people thought about them because they knew that they were better than everyone else. They knew that no one could even come close to being like them. They were unreachable; standing there high on the pedestals they were born on. But for a moment, I thought I was close. And in that brief moment, I felt like I had almost made it.

I remember when it happened, though. That night was warmer than it had been all week, and the sky was so clear that every star was shining brighter than I'd ever seen them shine before. Like when you're out in nature with no city lights to obstruct the view; it was that kind of clear. The night felt like magic was in the air. It was the kind of night that felt like all of your wishes could come true.

The moon was full, and the light it emitted hit the palm trees outside of my windows, creating a glow around them. The glow made them seem even more beautiful, yet frightening, all at the same time. Those palm trees; they stood taller in that light, like they were the protectors of Los Angeles in some weird way. They looked like they were giant shadows in the sky, looking down on me, letting me know that I was here, in the right place, in the right moment in time. I know that sounds ridiculous, but that's what they seemed like.

I had been home from my shift for about an hour when I heard a knock at my door. My heart began to race with excitement with the thought that it could possibly be Roxy on the other side, and maybe Dalton was with her. I didn't want to seem too eager, so I took my time answering.

That's when everything became a blur. I was ransacked back into my apartment; tape was put over my mouth and I was blindfolded. Sheer terror came over my whole body. I thought that I was going to be killed. Murdered. You hear stories like that, especially being a young, single woman, but when it's actually happening to you, the fear that comes over you is indescribable.

My attackers began to drag me out of my home—my safe place. They shoved me into the trunk of a car, and I had no sense of what was going on or where they were taking me. I only had my faith that my grandmother was watching over me and was going to keep me safe.

What seemed like an hour had passed when the car finally shut off. My heart was pounding. My entire body was shaking and convulsing with panic and absolute terror. Finally, I was taken out of the trunk and pushed from behind. My feet sank with every step, weighing me down as the familiar part of the earth filled my shoes. Then the salty, crisp air hit my nose and I knew where I was. The beach. But why?

After a good distance, I was shoved to the ground. My sight had been taken away, but my other senses had heightened, and I could feel a warmth coming over me. It was a feeling that I had felt before. Another familiar feeling that reminded me of when I was a kid, back home in a cold, Missouri winter. It was a comforting warmth—a warmth from fire. At that point, my head was spinning and nothing made sense. The thoughts in my head over-took anything else. Who had taken me? Why did they take me? What was going on? What was going to happen? Was I going to die? Then the blindfold was taken off.

My eyes had to adjust to the growing flames, and then I saw it. I saw them.

"What's going on?" I asked, terrified, not knowing what they were planning to do to me. I had only met them a few days prior.

"Initiation time, Baby! You ready for a swim?" the familiar voice said with a laugh.

"Sebastian?" I cried with relief.

"See, I told you she could handle it."

"Roxy?" It was her. I knew that gentle voice. "Is that you?"

"I asked you if you wanted to be our new member, but now you have to prove it," she said. As my eyes adjusted, I could see Roxy, Chad and Sebastian shuffling around. I tried to see what they were doing, and I tried to get up, but I couldn't.

I looked down at the sand with a wave of relief rushing over me. I took a deep breath. When I looked up, his eyes were staring at me. I could feel them burning a hole through my soul, almost as if he were trying to reach in and figure out everything about who I was. There was so much intensity in those eyes—those amazing eyes. They made me feel safe. They made me feel unafraid and calm. It was almost as if they were trying to tell me something; like they were letting me know that everything would be okay. That it would be okay because of him, because he was there. I didn't want him to take those eyes off of me. I couldn't take mine off of his, and I didn't want that feeling to go away. That feeling of being guarded, or protected. There was something in him; something that I wanted to see, to know more about. That mystery. That mystery that made me fall in love with him the second I first saw him. That mystery that would always be there, no matter how close we got, or not. It would always be there, like it was a little secret just for me.

"Here, drink this," Chad said, breaking the connection between Dalton and I.

"What is it?" I asked.

"Uh, Uh, Uh. I thought that you wanted to be one of us?" he snapped back.

I grabbed the drink from his hand and nearly spit it out. The taste in my mouth was awful. But for some reason, this potent substance that I could barely swallow was somehow what I needed to drink to get in with them —to be one of them. At least, that's what I told myself. I still didn't quite understand, but I drank it anyway.

I immediately looked up at Dalton for reassurance, but he wasn't there anymore. And when I started to look around for him, I was swooped up by Chad and Sebastian and led down to the water. I desperately wanted to be one of them, so I didn't try to put up a fight. I trusted them because I trusted Roxy, and I knew that she wouldn't let anything bad happen to me. She was my friend.

They dropped me just as we hit the water. I had grown dizzy somewhere along the way, and I couldn't stand up. My brain had suddenly lost control of my legs, just as more water was rushing over me. I got pulled back with the current and struggled to stay above the surface. The heaviness of my eyes made it almost impossible to stay conscious, but I remember seeing the four of them standing on dry land looking at me—watching me. I came to the realization that they weren't going to help. They were letting this happen. They wanted me to suffer.

And then he kissed her.

I tried shaking my head to hopefully help myself see clearly, but even with my fading vision and urge to fall asleep, I knew what I had seen. He kissed her, and she was kissing him back. She was playing me, *he* was playing me; they all were. One by one, each part of my body was losing the will to survive. When another giant wave toppled over me, I had to force my legs and arms to move to try to stay above water, but I couldn't. And when I tried to scream, nothing came out. I was going to die, and they were going to watch me.

I fought as hard as I could to breathe. I fought as hard as I could to stay alive. It wasn't my time yet, it couldn't be. I still had things that I wanted to accomplish, places that I needed to visit, and a person who I needed to become. I was trying so hard to move, to swim, to fight for my life, but nothing would budge, no matter how hard I tried. Once I couldn't fight anymore, I just closed my eyes and decided to let it happen. That would be it. It would all be over.

So much for my dream. So much for finally getting the chance to fit in.

Chapter Five

My head was throbbing like I'd been hit over and over again by a baseball bat, and my body wasn't in any better shape. My ribs felt like they'd been crushed to fragments, and my lungs were bruised from trying so hard to fight to breathe. I had a vague memory of what had happened the night before, but it seemed too bizarre to be true. Why would people that I call my friends do something so torturous to me? It didn't make any sense. It was a dream—a painful dream that felt real —it had to be. I mean, almost dying and having people there who could have saved me, but wouldn't; that only happened in movies or dreams, not in real life. It just doesn't, does it?

My beat-up body had a hard time getting out of bed, and after fighting with itself for a few minutes, I was finally able to get it moving. As I was slowly moving towards the kitchen, there was a knock at the door. My heart stopped. Images of my dream flashed in my head, making it practically impossible for my hand to reach for the doorknob. I wanted to run and hide, but instead I started shaking uncontrollably.

"Who is it?" I asked, my voice quivering, fearing the worst.

No answer.

"Who's there?" I yelled, too afraid to get close to the door.

Silence.

Every bone in my body was shaking at that point. I managed to turn the handle, and... nothing. No one was there.

I let out the little breath that I was keeping in and let myself relax. It had to have been some kid playing a prank on me. There were a couple of kids that lived a few doors down, so it seemed like the most logical explanation, but it was still nerve-wracking.

The door was starting to close when, "SURPRISE!" Roxy yelled while jumping in front of me.

I almost had a heart attack. "Roxy, you scared me half to death!" I said in a panic.

"You should've seen your face. Definitely a candid camera moment!" she said, laughing without remorse. "Can I come in?"

"Yeah, sorry. I'm just a little shaken up. I had a really bad dream last night, and I must not be over it."

"Bad dream?" she questioned. "What was it about?"

"Well, I must've fallen asleep when I got home from work yesterday, because my dream started from that exact point," I began telling her. "There was a knock at the door and these masked creatures blindfolded and attacked me. They threw me in the trunk of their car and took me to the beach. When they finally took the blindfold off of me, I saw you, Chad and Sebastian." Roxy was listening intently. "Then my dream took a strange turn. I was in the ocean and couldn't swim. By that time, Dalton had shown up and you and him were making out while I was drowning." I paused. "And I must've been tossing and turning because my whole body aches now."

Roxy was looking at me with a dead expression, and then she began to laugh.

"Why are you laughing? I was really scared. I still am. I felt like I was going to die!"

"You are too much, Jules! That, like, really happened! Except me making out with Dalton. That part *must* have been a dream." She continued to laugh.

I sat there, shocked, wondering how a friend dying— or in a sense, being murdered—could possibly be amusing to her. Some time passed of me listening to her haunting laughter. "Why would you almost let me drown?" I angrily asked. "Did you drug me or something because I blacked out and—"

"Don't worry about it. It was just our little way of welcoming you into our group." She tried to smooth things over. "It was just our way of accepting you as one of us, blah, blah, blah. We all did something stupid like that."

"Like what? Trying to kill each other?" My anger kept rising.

"No, what do you expect, to be some sort of collateral

damage?" she rudely questioned. "It just got a little out of hand," she brushed off.

"No, I just," I paused. "You guys really scared me is all. I really thought that I was going to die, Roxy," I said.

"Jules, I would never let that happen to you. You're like, my best friend."

"Really!?" I couldn't believe it. I had a best friend now, finally. Everything that had happened the night before completely vanquished from my mind, almost like it didn't happen at all. And that kiss? Roxy herself said that it didn't happen. So that part was definitely just in my head. Roxy was my best friend, and she would never let anything bad happen to me. She said so herself.

"You're my best friend too, Roxy!" I was relieved, and all of my nerves disappeared.

We hugged, my best friend and me. She smelled of strawberry lip gloss and expensive perfume. It was always nothing but the best for Roxy Harrington. Her beauty was that of one of my favorite movie stars—timeless—and she was perfect in every way, from her smile to the things she said. She was my best friend.

"So, Dalton told me that he couldn't keep his eyes off of you last night," she said, smirking at me.

"What? Really?" I said, beaming.

"Yeah, he said that he was going to call you either today or tomorrow and ask you out."

"Oh, that's cool." I tried to play it off.

"Cool? Oh, come on Jules, it's me. Just admit that you love him," she pressured.

She *was* my best friend. "Okay, fine. He is totally rad, and so sexy," I admitted.

"I knew it!" she exclaimed.

"How?"

"Because you basically glaze over whenever you see him or we talk about him, duh!"

Was it that obvious? Did Dalton know? He's supposed to be asking me out, does he feel the same way? Those were the only thoughts running through my mind.

Roxy and I talked for another hour while I iced my aching ribs. We were laughing about some story she was telling me about Sebastian when all of a sudden she became silent and looked at me. She slowly smiled and said, "You know Jules, I've never had a friend I could truly be myself with. I'm so glad that we met."

I smiled back, so happy that she was in my life. "Me too." That's when I realized that the soreness that my body was experiencing was now more of a good sore; a well-deserved sore. Because Roxy was more than a friend. More than a best friend, even. She was a true friend, and those don't always come by that easily.

Before Roxy left, she told me that the group was planning to go out and celebrate my "initiation." She said that the coming Saturday night I should meet her at Dalton's at 6 p.m. to get ready together. I was so excited, I couldn't wait.

An hour after she left, I had to go to work. I was still in pain, but I didn't want Jeffery and Dawson to find out what had happened to me the night before, so I took two aspirin and sucked it up to keep it on the downlow.

After my shift, Dawson asked me if I wanted to go out for drinks. "Come on, we can gossip. I feel like I haven't seen you much lately."

I turned him down. I was more eager to sit by the phone and wait for Dalton to call me about our date. I felt bad for ditching one of my first friends in LA, but now that I was in "the group," Dawson just wasn't that important to me anymore. I had already impressed him and Jeffery, but I still had to impress Dalton and Roxy to solidify myself as one of them. And they were, honestly, more fun to hang out with. You never knew what the night had in store for you when you were with them.

He didn't call that night.

I had the next day off and my only plan was to sit by the phone and wait for that call. I didn't want to miss it. I was watching some Sally Jessy Raphael when there was a knock on my door. My heart skipped a little beat not knowing what, or who, could be on the other side. But I was already a part of them, so I knew I didn't have anything to be afraid of.

"What are you guys doing here?" I asked in bewilderment.

"We were just in the neighborhood. Wanted to stop by and say hi," Chad smiled.

"Do you guys want to come in?" I gestured.

"Yeah, I'm thirsty." Sebastian walked right in past me.

"I have water or juice."

"Anything stronger?" he remarked.

"No, sorry," I shrugged.

"That sucks. Water I guess."

"Hey, this is a great place Jules," Chad said, settling down onto my couch, making himself comfortable.

"Thanks," I yelled from the kitchen.

Of course, Sebastian had to leave his mark on the topic. "It's kinda small."

"At least she has her own place."

"Yeah, don't you still live at home with your parents?" I asked him, handing them each a glass of water before sitting down in my armchair.

"Whatever. You guys are lame."

"Can I smoke in here?"

"Umm, no sorry. I just don't really want..."

"It's cool," Chad said. "So, do you like it here? It has to be better than wherever you're from, right?"

It was kind of nice hearing Chad taking an interest in me. I hadn't really talked much with him before, and this unexpected visit made me start to notice just how charming he was. He didn't make your heart start to race, but he was sweet. I could see what girls liked about him. "Missouri, and yeah. I'm really liking it so far. Loving it, actually. I mean, I did think about going home a while back, but..." I paused. "I don't know. I have Roxy and you guys now, so..."

"And Dalton," Sebastian said in a lovey dovey way.

I couldn't hold back the instant rush of blood to my cheeks. "Yeah, and Dalton," I smirked. "You guys make LA feel like home now."

"Good, 'cause we like you too." Chad smiled.

"Yeah, you make things more fun." Sebastian took a sip of his water.

"Really?" I questioned. "That's nice of you to say. But how do I do that?" I laughed.

He shrugged. "You make Roxy nicer."

That was a strange comment coming from him, but it was Sebastian; he always said random things without thinking. Roxy always appeared to be the nicest, most caring friend when she was around me. I know that we weren't always around each other, but she just couldn't be any other way. She was... perfect. I couldn't see her being mean to anyone. She always had a smile on her face and yes, she could be blunt, but that didn't make her a bad person. I brushed off his remark, thinking he was just being Sebastian.

"No, dude. Yeah, you're right," Chad said to him before turning towards me. "You do make her nicer. Like way less of a bitch. She's always been like that but she's different when you're around."

I didn't quite know how to reply to that comment, so I just said, "Well, I love Roxy, so I guess that's good."

"Yeah, but you really love Dalton, dontcha?" Sebastian nodded in my direction.

My cheeks began to burn, along with the uncomfortable smile plastered to my face.

"It's okay, don't pay attention to him. Dalton's a good guy. We've known him forever, he's just... Dalton."

"Speaking of Dalton," Sebastian interrupted. "Let's head over there. I'm bored and I need some refreshments."

"Yeah, okay. Bye Jules, see ya later," Chad said, standing up before giving me a hug.

"Thanks for the water," Sebastian said extending his arm for a high five.

After they left, I went back to my waiting. He didn't call that night either. That third night though—that third night, he called and asked to pick me up in an hour. I scrambled to call Jeffery and asked him to cover my shift, which he gladly did. Then I frantically got ready for a date that I was hoping would change my life forever.

Chapter Six

At 7 p.m., Dalton knocked on my door. It surprised me that I was able to answer with shocking ease, because everything in me was shaking from nerves.

"Hey gorgeous! You ready to go?" he asked, so perfectly. I could have just melted right then and there.

"Yeah, let me just grab my purse." I smiled, with a cute little bite to my lip.

We walked out of my building and he opened the passenger door for me. It was a simple gesture, but it made him seem all the more gentlemanly; a part of men that seemed to be starting to fade.

"So, you said that you've been to some bars, right?"

"Oh, you remembered?" I asked, surprised that he had.

"I don't forget things from important people," he said, with one side of his mouth ever so cocked. I blushed and smiled back. You know the kind of flirty, shy smile where you're trying to be cute, but inside you're freaking out with excitement? That's how he made me feel; like anything was possible.

These were signals, right? He had to have liked me. As we drove away from my apartment, he started to play some music. Guns N' Roses. To be exact, Sweet Child O'Mine. They were his favorite band, and they were the perfect soundtrack for our date.

We drove with the windows down, letting the wind blow through our hair, hitting our faces and making every strum of the guitar electrify the night even more. I was feeling a whirlwind of emotions, spanning from pure happiness, to relaxation, to the most excited that you could possibly be when you're out with your dream guy for the first time. I remember holding my hand out of the window, letting the warm air rush past my fingertips. Every brush of air on my skin made me feel like I was the luckiest girl in the world.

"Where to first?" he asked me.

"I thought that *you* were going to show *me* around?" I coyly said.

"True. Maybe I was thinking out loud," he smiled along with the guitar solo playing through the speakers, as if it was his time to shine. I don't know, Dalton had a way of making things feel like an experience; like it wasn't happening at all, but you were there anyway. He made you feel like a part of it and more in the moment.

We kept driving until we were driving through the hills and got to the Griffith Observatory.

"This is *the* spot in LA for seeing the whole city," he said.

"It's beautiful," I said back, taking in the view.

"Yeah, over there is Downtown and below us is Hollywood Boulevard. And way out in that direction is Malibu. We'll have to go there one day. Roxy's family has a house out there. We'll make it a beach day."

"That sounds perfect."

"But I saved the best for last." He began turning me in the direction of the most beautiful sight.

It was the Hollywood sign, as close as I'd ever been and absolutely breathtaking. "Oh, Dalton! It's beautiful!"

"I knew that you'd love this. It's your dream, right? So, I brought you a little closer to it."

I didn't think it was possible to fall more in love with someone I barely even knew, but it wasn't just anyone. It was definitely possible to fall more in love with Dalton Blake. And that night, in that moment, I did. This guy who had a hold on me, who looked at me in a way that only someone who really loved you would. I was in love with him.

We got back into his car and headed back down the hill, where we began to drive down Sunset Boulevard.

"Did Roxy tell you that we're going out on Saturday?"

"Yeah, she said to meet at your place around 9."

"Cool," he said, and then kept quiet for about a minute, before finally continuing. "We usually go out on the strip. It's the scene right now. It was big in the '80's for all of the hair bands, but it's still got its charm about it. I'm not sure where we're going, but that's my favorite place right there," he said, pointing to The Viper Room. "Have you been there yet?"

"No, I actually haven't been anywhere on the strip yet."

"Really? Who's been taking you out?" Dalton asked, curiously.

"These two guys from work. We've just been going to bars."

"Two guys, huh? Are you seeing either of them?" he asked, seeming eager for my answer to be no.

I laughed a little. "No, they're gay."

"Okay good," he said. "I can't have other guys around my girl."

"Your girl?" I asked, looking at him with my eyebrow raised and a playful smirk across my face, genuinely curious.

He just looked into my eyes and grinned, before looking back at the road.

What was that supposed to mean? How could he just give me that sexy look without a single word? Was he interested in me? He had to be, right? Did this mean that we were dating? I've only ever had two boyfriends before, and they weren't anything like Dalton. They were small town boys, and their idea of a fancy date was going to the diner I worked at. They weren't the best at flirting or leading a girl on. They said things as is, so why wouldn't Dalton just say so? Or was it all a part of the mystery behind Dalton Blake? Whatever it was, I liked it. It made me nervous, but it felt good, and it felt right. All I could do was smile, in that butterflies-in-your-stomach kind of way, and look out the window.

We kept driving on Sunset until we were in Beverly Hills. We veered off to the right and entered The Beverly Hills Hotel.

The valet opened the doors and greeted us. "Hello, Mr. Blake. It's nice to see you again."

"Hey John, how are you?" Dalton politely responded.

"Great, sir. How are things with you?"

"Couldn't be better," he said, smiling and looking at me. "Actually," he pulled me in close to him, "Better than perfect. I've got a beautiful girl on my arm, what more could a guy ask for?"

"That's great, Mr. Blake. Enjoy your night."

"Yeah, thank you. Oh, and John, it's Dalton. Mr. Blake's my father," he said, pointing at John.

How perfect was he? He was dashing and charming. He knew exactly what to say at all times to everyone. He kept on exceeding my expectations and making me feel so special, like I was the only girl in the world—*his* only girl.

Dalton looked at me and smiled, then we proceeded to walk inside. That's when I started to panic a little bit. This was a hotel—a fancy hotel. As much as I was in love with Dalton Blake, I wasn't ready to go to a room with him. My heart began pounding and I was beginning to feel sick to my stomach. Did Dalton really think that I was going to be that easy? I mean, a few sly looks, taking me to my dream, and saying so much without saying anything at all? That didn't make me ready.

We walked past the check-in desk and down a small hallway to a restaurant door. My nerves suddenly disappeared. Dinner. He was taking me to dinner. I should have known better. The way he was treating me wasn't how people described him. He wasn't being that playboy I had heard someone say in passing. He was sweet and respectful.

We got a table right away, even though it was packed. A few of the patrons said hello to Dalton as we were escorted past them to a table on the outside patio.

"Don't tell Roxy or the guys that I took you here. No one knows that I come here," he said, looking deeply into my eyes, like he had done that night on the beach.

"I promise, I won't."

"Good." He paused and looked around. "This is my favorite place in all of LA."

"And you brought *me* here?" I asked.

"I know I can trust you," he winked. "You're a good girl, not like the girls you find running around this city."

"Beverly Hills? Or Los Angeles in general?" I asked, with a cute little raise of my eyebrow.

He laughed. "In general."

I looked at him and smiled.

"So, tell me, why is this your favorite place?"

"Because it's quiet."

"Really?" I questioned, looking around. "It looks like it's at capacity. There were even people waiting at the door," I pointed out.

"You're so funny, Julie," he said with a little laugh. "I mean quiet as in, kind of hush hush. No one tells anyone that they saw you at The Polo Lounge."

"Oh," I said, feeling embarrassed.

"It's okay. This could be *our* spot," he said.

"Okay!" I answered, not reading into what that meant. If no one told anyone that they saw you here and this was our spot, were we not supposed to be seen together? But of course, I was—and still am—so in love with Dalton Blake that the thought went right out of my head. I mean, I was *his girl*. Right?

From there, the night kept getting better. We ate the most incredible dinner and had the most amazing chocolate soufflé. Then we were off to our next destination.

The drive was long, but every second with Dalton was perfect. I had to try and not just sit there and stare at him, which was really hard to do. So, I looked out my window and let the wind and the music take over every part of me. Every now and then, he would point out a building or landmark and tell me what it was and if *we* would ever go there together.

After a while, we ended up in Venice Beach and walked around. The breeze from the ocean started to pick up, and I began to shiver. It didn't seem like it would be that cold. Dalton put his leather jacket around me, and then his arm. I melted into him, breathing in his scent and feeling like I could live in that moment forever.

"Are you warm enough?" he asked.

"Yes, thank you Dalton," I said, gazing into his eyes. God, those eyes. I still see them every time I think about him. They were the type of eyes that had a little bit of extra light in them. They type of eyes that only someone really special has.

We came to an open spot and sat against a palm tree. I was leaning against Dalton with his arms wrapped around me. I was in heaven. I looked up at him, and that's when he kissed me. That kiss was exactly how I'd imagined it would be. Those soft, sultry lips gently, yet with some force, pressed against mine. I could feel the warmth of his breath against my face as our tongues gently grazed over each other's. I didn't want his lips to ever come off of me. Maybe we were more than I was hoping we were. Maybe we were more than the group. Maybe we were *actually* falling in love. Maybe I wasn't the secret that I thought I was.

Dalton was a perfect gentleman. He completely surprised me. I thought that he was going to be a typical pretty boy, kind of like Chad and Sebastian, and try to sleep with me and never call me again. But he opened my car door, took me to his favorite spots around town, offered me his jacket when I was cold, and kissed me. It was the perfect date.

My perception upon meeting him was greatly altered with the knowledge of this hidden "good boy" that was in him, which made him seem all the more... bad. When he walked me to my door, he didn't try to come in. He stood there, holding my hand and pulling me in closer to him.

"I had a good time tonight, Julie," he said.

"I did too! Thank you, Dalton! And, you can call me Jules."

"No," he paused. "You're my Julie." Then he kissed me and walked away.

He had me. I wasn't Jules from Westwood to him. I was Julie. Just Julie. I was me.

Chapter Seven

It was the big day—the "big night out." The night we would be celebrating *me*. It was going to be a great night, especially because of everything that was happening with me and Dalton. It was going to be an unforgettable night. I just knew it. I had asked to have the early shift so that I would have time to shower before heading over to his house to get ready with Roxy. It was the longest day, counting down the hours until I could see Dalton and kiss his irresistible lips again. He hadn't called me since our date a few nights before, but it was LA, and he was... him. I figured that's what they did here; leave you hanging and wanting more.

Jeffery was working the same shift as I was, which we hadn't done in a while. He asked me if I wanted to go out after work, but I turned him down again.

"What's up with you, Julie?" he asked with a sad, disappointed tone underlying his voice. "Why've you been flaking on me and Dawson so much lately?" he asked, point blank.

"I've just been busy with work and auditioning," I lied. He probably knew it too, because I usually told him about all of my auditions. Truthfully, since the Richard Harrington one, I hadn't gone on any others.

"Well, just don't forget who *really* loves you," he said.

"Jeffery, how could I? You and Dawson are my best friends." I lied again.

"Just be careful, Julie." There was a look of worry in his eyes. It was almost as if he was warning me.

"I will! You don't have to worry about me." I smiled and walked away.

I avoided him for the rest of our shift. I remember feeling annoyed with him; like when you get mad at someone who's being nosy and wants to know your business. You just get put off by them. I started to feel like I didn't want to talk to him anymore. Besides, I had new friends. Friends that liked me and wanted me to hang out with them so badly that they would do *anything* to make that happen. Like almost killing me.

When my shift was over, I raced home and took a shower. I quickly packed my makeup and an outfit and headed over to Dalton's.

His house was beautiful. I don't think I mentioned that before. Upon pulling up, I saw his Chevelle and Chad's BMW, but I didn't see Roxy's Mercedes. My heart was racing. Roxy was my in, my best friend, and my key to these guys. We did briefly hangout that one time when they showed up at my place, but what would I even talk to them about? I mean, I was still so nervous around Dalton, even though we had just gone out and had the most perfect night. He made me nervous, in a good way, and gave me butterflies. He made me giddy even, as lame as that sounds.

I decided to take my time getting my things out of my car when, "Finally!" her familiar, beautiful voice exclaimed.

"Oh, I figured you weren't here yet. I didn't see your car," I said, nervously.

"The boys picked me up," she said casually. "We've been waiting for you, Jules. Come on, I need your help picking out my outfit!"

We went inside and I said hello to Chad and Sebastian, who were sitting on the couch watching music videos on MTV. Dalton wasn't anywhere that I could see.

"Is Dalton here?" I asked, maybe a little too eagerly.

"Ooooh, Dalton!" Sebastian said in a sarcastic way. "Somebody's in love!" he exclaimed, leaning over to Chad, making a kissing sound.

"No, I was just..."

"Don't listen to him Jules, he's high," Roxy said, grabbing my arm and pulling me away.

High? That terrible feeling in the pit of my stomach started to kick in. Was Sebastian doing drugs? What was I getting myself into? I was raised to never touch the stuff. Let's just say the D.A.R.E. program worked on me—"*Just say no!*" I mean, I knew that there were different kinds of drugs out there, but I had no idea what they did. I just knew that they were bad—very bad—and that I shouldn't touch them.

"Is this too boring?" Roxy asked, stepping out of the closet.

"No, you look great!" I responded.

I couldn't help but notice that the room was a mess. There were clothes strewn all over the place: the floor, the bed, everywhere. This was Dalton's house. Why was Roxy being so disrespectful by not putting her things back in her bag? It seemed so rude and inconsiderate of her, but Roxy could get away with anything. She always did what she wanted, and no one ever questioned her. That's the kind of power and presence she had. She was untouchable.

"So, is this Dalton's room?" I curiously asked her, but she didn't answer. Instead, she walked out of the closet in a little black dress that was, honestly, to die for. "That's it! That's the one you should wear, it's gorgeous!" I said.

"I know! It just came in this morning. I hope the guys will like it."

"Of course, they will! You look stunning," I said, turning to look at my own self in the mirror. "I, on the other hand, look..."

"Yeah, no offense, I hate your outfit," Roxy quipped.

No one had ever been that blunt towards me before. What she said was mean and my feelings were a little hurt, but she was my best friend. That's what best friends are supposed to do, right? Look out for you? Make sure you look your best?

"Here, this might fit you," she said, handing me a slinky little black number.

I tried on the barely-there dress and looked at the new me in the mirror.

"Hot! Definitely what you should wear tonight," Roxy said.

"I don't know, it's not really me."

"Dalton's going to love it!" she said, reassuringly.

"He will?"

"He won't be able to keep his hands off of you." She smiled and then headed towards the door. "Come on, Jules! We have to get downstairs; the guys are waiting. By the way, how was your date with Dalton?"

"Perfect!" I said, blushing. "He kissed me!"

"What? No way!" she said, sounding a little surprised. "He so likes you!"

"You think?" I said as I gazed at myself in the mirror once more before leaving Dalton's room. This was me. Jules from Westwood, but Dalton's Julie.

When we got downstairs, Dalton had joined the guys who were huddled around the coffee table. "Rox, Jules, you've got to get in on this," Sebastian yelled over to us.

As we approached, I was curious to see what they were doing, what they were so excited about. I had a bad feeling—a feeling that I knew I wasn't going to like whatever it was they were huddled around. But I went over anyways.

"Who scored?" Roxy asked, squeezing herself between the two guys.

"Rox, did you even need to ask?" Chad answered.

"Right," she laughed.

I stood there in shock. I knew that these entitled people did whatever they wanted, but hardcore drugs were the furthest thing from my mind when I thought of possibilities. Sex, I knew they did. Pot, I had found out earlier, but these drugs? Pills? No.

Dalton saw that I was standoffish and walked over to me. "Jules, are you okay?"

"I'm fine," I smiled.

"We have one left Jules, and it's got your name on it." Sebastian held it out towards me.

"It's okay, it won't hurt you. If anything, it'll make you feel better," Dalton said, slowly rubbing his hand up and down my back as he whispered, "Julie, do you trust me?"

He said it. The words that would change my life forever. I had fallen in love with Dalton in the short amount of time that we had known one another. He had the irresistible face of an angel, and the cool, smoldering heart of the devil. How could I not trust him? He was the one. The guy that every girl wished wanted her, and he was mine.

"I do," I said, gazing into his soft, cool eyes.

"Just stick with me tonight. You'll be fine," he reassured.

Sebastian walked towards me with the little pill that I feared so much in that moment. Not knowing what this little, tiny, thing would do to me was terrifying enough, but I also had my grandmother's voice in the back of my mind; telling me that it was wrong, telling me to stay awake, to be aware. But I did it anyway.

"Welcome to the ecstasy club, Jules, it only gets better from here!" Sebastian said.

"Okay! Let's go!" Roxy screamed with excitement.

As we were heading towards the door, Dalton caught my arm and pulled me back into the living room. He brought me in close to him and started to kiss me.

"You look absolutely beautiful tonight." His voice hummed out the notes as he gave me a look; a look that I knew meant he wanted me. Then he brought his lips to mine once more, but only for a quick moment before he stopped to brush a strand of hair softly from my face, without ever taking his eyes off of mine. "You do incredible things to me, Julie," he whispered.

He began to gently caress his hand down my face to my neck, and then down the front of my body until he reached my hand. He grabbed it, and then we walked out the door.

Chapter Eight

Sunset Boulevard was beautiful on this particular night. The weather was perfect, with just a touch of a tiny chill, but nothing too drastic for LA for the time of the year. I remember feeling like my body and mind were set free from everything bad that had ever happened in my life. I felt happy and relaxed. I could feel everything; from the cool, crisp wind hitting my face to the heat that was coursing through my veins as Roxy and I hung out of the windows. It felt like everything was how it was supposed to be. When you're young and really don't have a care in the world. It almost felt like I was flying, like a bird, gracefully gliding through the sky. Free. I was flying, and no one was going to let me fall. If that was how drugs could make you feel, then why had I been so afraid? I felt great. My life was great, and nothing would make me think otherwise.

The music in the car was blaring, but I could hardly hear a sound. The lights on the Sunset Strip were shining as bright as they ever would be, but I could barely see the words the neon letters made. It was real; this life that I always imagined that I would have, with the kind of people I always wanted around me. It was real.

"Get back in, Jules," Sebastian said, pulling me back through the window.

"What were you girls even doing?" Chad yelled over the music blasting from the speakers.

"Thinking about doing this," Roxy said before she started to make out with Sebastian and then moved on to make out with Chad, even though he was driving.

The car began to swerve into the other lane. Horns and headlights flashed in front of my screaming face before Dalton pulled her off of Chad.

There was a silence that came over us all until, "Flying."

"What did you say, Jules?" Chad asked, laughing.

"I was flying," I replied.

"Okay. How high?" Roxy asked behind her laughter.

"As high as the palm trees," I said in a daze.

"The palm trees, huh?" Sebastian smirked. "Is she always gonna be like this?" he pointed at me. "I like it," he answered his own question, putting his arm around me, pulling me in. "Jules, you and I are gonna be best buds. You hear me?"

"You know what? I do, Sebastian. I do hear you."

Sebastian and I had bonded in a very unexpected way.

∽

We pulled up to a crowd of people hanging around and waiting to get into The Viper Room. We somehow arrived unscathed from Chad's ecstasy and make out induced driving.

Dalton grabbed my hand and helped me out of the car. I thought that it was a little strange that he wasn't very affectionate with me at his house in front of everyone. He had only been affectionate with me privately. I figured that he was trying to play it cool. But I don't know what I was higher from: the ecstasy, or that kiss with his lingering affection. He put his arm around me, and we walked into the club like we were celebrities. Everyone's eyes were on us, but really, we looked more like a couple, and I don't think people expected that from him. We were the only two people that mattered in that moment, and that was something I wasn't going to ever let slip away.

With everyone's eyes on us, it made the night even more exciting. It was a mesmerizing experience; something I always dreamed of when I thought about my future as an actress. It was Dalton though; it couldn't have been me. I was a nobody; he was Dalton Blake. Everyone in that scene knew who he was and thought of him as this untouchable icon, this so-called sex God that girls across the city pinned him as. I mean, what more could I say? He was a legend in his own right, and he could get *anybody*. But he wanted *me*.

The club was crowded. I really had never seen anything like it. The smoke-filled air felt thrilling and vibrant, and the people standing around let off a cool vibe, as if they were setting the tone of how the evening would play out. You could feel the sounds of the guitars beaming out of the amps, which made them roll through my ears, allowing me to feel every strum of the axe. I was a different person surrounded by everything in there. It was like the music ran through my soul and set it on fire. I was Jules, no longer Julie. I was the new me; the more outgoing me. The me that let this city bury itself deep inside of my heart, where it was going to be locked inside forever. There was no way I would ever turn back on it now, not with everything that was happening. Missouri was now just a distant memory.

Dalton's arm—that strong arm—was still around me, and I could feel the envious eyes of the ones he had passed over glued to me. In some surreal way, I felt like I had made it. I was the star that I was destined to be. He made me feel that way; like my dreams were coming true. And with Dalton in my life, I *had* made it. I realized that no matter what the future held for my career, he was all I needed, and all I ever wanted.

"This is incredible!" I yelled over the bass.

"Yeah, it's okay. It hasn't been open for too long," Roxy said. "Chad, I want to say hi to Johnny. Tell me if you see him."

"Who's Johnny?" I asked.

"Oh, a family friend. He co-owns this place," Roxy shrugged, nonchalantly.

Again, she had me shocked. Who knows the owners of clubs? It always blew my mind just how intriguing these people were, and they were my friends. I kept being drawn in more and more with every move that they made. How was this real? How were people like this? So glamorous. So dreamlike. I almost had to pinch myself to make sure that I was actually living this life.

"Here," Sebastian said, handing me a drink.

"Thank you!" I yelled.

The drink was strong. I'm not even sure what it really was, but it tasted strange. Not that I had a lot of alcohol in my life. I usually kept it simple when I did drink; a glass of wine or a beer, nothing fancy. I just figured that the ecstasy I had taken could have impaired some of my senses, so I relaxed and let the music take over as I danced and danced.

After that, the night became a blur. The music was loud—so loud that I couldn't hear anything else, let alone my own thoughts. We just kept moving. I had never felt so loose and free before. All of my inhibitions and anxieties went away for what felt like hours. But who knows, it could have only been minutes or seconds.

The night continued to rage on, with more drinks and more dancing. The more I felt myself loosening up, the more alive I began to feel. The extreme shyness and the ever-present feeling that I was never truly enough melted away. I was carefree and enjoying every minute of my life. But then, a dark figure started approaching me and that natural panic came over me once again. All I could think to do was to reach for Dalton—to reach for those arms that I felt so comfortable in. The arms that made me feel nervous and safe all at the same time. I just wanted to pull him in closer and feel his lips against mine.

But he wasn't there.

"Dalton!" I screamed. "Dalton!"

Nothing.

I turned around quickly to look for him; for any of them.

Nothing. No one.

And then everything went dark.

Chapter Nine

I woke up to excruciating pain. My head felt like it had exploded. It was throbbing so badly, it was hard to focus my eyes. I had to struggle to keep them open, but when I did, I didn't recognize the room that I was in. I was so dizzy and could barely breathe, with waves of nausea flooding over me. I just wanted to go home.

As I slowly got up, I noticed something strange next to me on the bed.

Blood.

That alarmed me, so I looked around the trashed room, panicked, but found that I was alone. I started crying, which made the throbbing worse. Everything in me had vanquished from my body; every breath that I was holding onto, every scream I was holding in, every part of me that was just, holding on. I was scared and had no memory of what had happened. The entire night was blank, almost as if it *didn't* happen. I had to get out, I had to leave. All I could think was that the worst possible thing that I could have ever imagined happening to me, had happened to me.

I was terrified and couldn't help but think, *What if the person that did this to me came back?* I couldn't face them. They had already taken so much from me. What if they hurt me even more?

My clothes were on the other side of the room. Looking at them kept making them appear further and further away. Kind of like what you see in a movie, where a hallway just keeps getting longer and longer. Once I mustered up the courage, I ran to get them, got dressed as fast as I could, and left.

Tears were pouring down my face. I felt so ashamed of myself, and disgusted that I could let something like this happen to me. I actually didn't even know *what* happened, that's the thing. I just knew that something wasn't right. Something bad was lingering over me; something that I knew I couldn't fix.

As I was walking across the lobby, a woman at the front desk called over to me. "Excuse me, Miss?"

I froze. I was terrified. I thought that, somehow, I would be in trouble for whatever happened. Or if something—anything—bad was going on, that she would think I was a part of it. But when I approached the desk, the woman smiled.

"Here, these are for you," she said, handing me a bouquet of red roses. "They're from the gentleman you were with last night."

With my hands shaking, I slowly grabbed the

bouquet from the woman. Attached to a red ribbon was a note. It read, *Thanks for the good time, Jules.*

Tears began streaming down my face. "What's wrong?" the woman asked. "Is everything alright?"

I was shaking all over. Who was this person that I couldn't remember? Was it Dalton? And if it was him, why would I be feeling this way? I honestly couldn't remember a thing. The last thing that I could recall was calling out for him, and then feeling a heavy grip around my arm. But he wouldn't do this to me. He cared about me. He was different. Or was he?

How could I even ask if the woman knew who this person was? I was embarrassed and a mess, and who knows what she thought about me standing in a panic in front of her. But I had to find out.

"Do you," I paused before continuing, "happen to know who it was?" I tried to hold back every bit of the fearful emotions I had.

"No, sorry, Ms. Simon, the room was under your name," she answered.

I began to hyperventilate.

"Are you alright? Do you need me to call an ambulance or the police?" she asked.

How could I go anywhere or tell anyone what had happened? I didn't even know what happened, and with everything that had gone on at the beach, and now this? Who was going to believe me? It all seemed so unreal. It could have been anyone with me last night: one of the guys, Dalton, or even a stranger. My life was playing out like a horror film. It was becoming this huge, frightening thing that I had to live in every day. It was almost as if it were stuck on repeat, with every bad thing continuously playing out in my head. In reality, it was rocking me back and forth, like one of my palm trees swaying in the wind.

I ran out of the hotel with desperation for answers and a strong urgency to get home. I jumped into the first taxi that I could find, and I cried the entire way home. Home. My own personal place to feel safe, you would think.

When I got to my door, it wasn't shut all the way. I remembered locking it before I headed over to Dalton's the evening before. I always made sure to double check, because my grandmother always did. It was a habit. I slowly pushed the door open and found that someone had broken in and destroyed everything. Furniture was knocked over, papers that I had in drawers were all over the place, and a photo of my grandmother and I was smashed on the ground. My safe place was now destroyed.

All I could think was, *Why was this happening to me? What did I do to deserve all of this? And why did bad things just follow me around?* There had to be some sort of explanation. My world felt like it was caving in; like that night on the beach where the waves were crashing over me, and no matter how hard I tried, I couldn't get out. The weight of the water holding me down with the tide, pulling me under and thrashing me around was a constant feeling in my chest, on an everyday basis these days.

I sank to the floor, sobbing, hugging my knees tightly

into my chest, and rocking back and forth. I needed my friend—my best friend. I got the strength to stand up and call Roxy. She was the only one that I could think of to call in that time of need, because she was my best friend and would be there for me. She would believe me. I needed her.

"Come over now," was all she said before hanging up the phone.

Somehow, I managed to get there. Somehow, I was able to change clothes and dial for a taxi to come and get me. Somehow—just somehow.

"Tell me what happened so we can figure out who did this to you," she said as she consoled me.

Breathe, just breathe. My mind was all over the place and I was the most terrified that I had ever been in in my life. I could hardly manage to get any words out of my mouth. My mind couldn't even come up with a sentence, no matter how big or little it was. When I was finally able to speak, all I could say was, "Why did this happen to me?"

Roxy hugged me and told me that everything would be okay, just like a best friend should do.

"There was a note," I said between my sobs. "With the flowers. Maybe you might recognize the writing or where it's from or something?" I asked, hopeful.

I showed the chilling note to my best friend, but she couldn't place it. "I don't recognize the shop and I'm not really good with recognizing handwriting. Usually it's whoever is taking the call that writes it if the sender doesn't go in themselves. But I do know that I've defi-nitely never seen this writing before."

"Will you take me to the police?" I asked her.

"No, Jules, you can't go to the police," she snapped.

I was taken aback by the quickness to her response. It was odd.

"What do you mean I can't go to the police? I have to!" I cried.

"Jules, they won't believe you. Come on, two crazy things happening to one person in one night? They would laugh at you and think that you were crazy," she said.

"But Roxy..."

"And besides. If this got out, which it probably would, it could hurt my father's reputation. And don't you want my father to cast you in a role? Something like this *cannot* be filed."

What? It didn't make any sense that my best friend wasn't supporting me. I could have gotten killed in either incident, but she didn't seem to think that this was as important as her father's reputation. I did want to get cast in a role by the famous "Richard Harrington," but what was more important? My safety? Or my career?

"Okay. I guess you're right," I paused. "I'm just so scared." I started to sob again.

"Which is why you're staying here with me for a few days, just so that I know that you're safe," she squeezed my hand.

"Roxy, you don't have to do that."

"Of course, I do. You're my best friend. I love you,

Jules." She smiled. "And besides, this way we can gossip about how much Dalton is worried about you."

"What? He told you that?"

"Yeah, I called him before you got here and told him about the break in, and well, he said that he hoped that you were okay. And hey, I saw you two at the club last night. He is *so* into you."

My heart instantly started feeling better. I knew that we were going somewhere after our date. Maybe I could put all of this behind me and move on towards a brighter future. A future that included me and Dalton, together.

Chapter Ten

While I was staying with Roxy, we were getting to know each other more and blossoming our friendship. She was so sweet to be taking care of me and trying to keep my mind off of what had happened. Having someone look out for me made it feel like I had family again; someone to rely on, someone that would always be there.

Thankfully, her father was out of town. It would have been awful for him to see me like that. He would definitely never cast me then; I'd be the girl who couldn't get anything right. The girl who couldn't make it for herself. The girl who'd never live up to her potential. I'd just be lost amongst the sea of others that once had a dream, and I didn't want him to see me like that. I wanted him to think that I could be the next big star in one of his movies. So having this time to get myself together, with the help of Roxy, was just what I needed, and she couldn't have been a better friend.

During my stay, we did the sort of things you dream about doing with your best friend as a kid. Although, she had been doing them all her life. She took me to get my hair and nails done. We went shopping on Rodeo and out to fabulous lunches. We saw a movie, got dressed up for dinners at her house that her chef made, and grubbed out on candy and ice cream.

On the third day of my stay, Roxy said that she had an appointment to go to and would be back the following afternoon. I didn't think much of it. I didn't need to ask where she was going. She had been so nice and hospitable to me; I didn't feel like she was trying to get rid of me or anything, but I did try to go home. Roxy insisted that I stay and that she would try and hurry back.

I was laying out by the pool, trying to finish a book that I had been reading for a while, when a shadow fell upon me. Startled, I sat up, nearly falling out of the lounge chair.

"Julie!" It was him. "Julie, Julie, I'm sorry. I didn't mean to scare you," he said, sitting down to hug me. "I'm so sorry, are you okay?" He sounded worried as he kissed my head and held on to me tightly.

"Yeah, I'm fine. I've just been a little jumpy lately." I tried to brush it off.

"Well, it's okay. I'm here now," he said, still holding me with his strong arms.

Breathing in his scent—my favorite scent—and feeling his warm body against mine helped relax my racing heart and calm me down.

"Did Roxy tell you to come over here?" I asked,

hoping that Roxy hadn't told him what had *fully* happened to me.

"No, I'm actually not talking to her right now. I just wanted to come and see you," he paused. "I missed you."

"I missed you too, Dalton." My heart was exploding with love for him, for Dalton—my Dalton. He made everything feel fine; better even, like nothing bad had even happened at all.

I smiled at him and he gently began to kiss me, but then he pulled away. "So how long is she gonna be gone for?"

"Until tomorrow afternoon," I said, wanting him to kiss me again. "How did you know that she was gone?"

"Sebastian."

"Right," I smirked.

His sultry eyes looked into mine. "I want to spend as long as I can with you, Julie."

"I want that too," I said back, looking from his eyes to his lips. He smiled and leaned in, our mouths meeting for another kiss. I can't even begin to explain just how good his lips felt when they were on mine. When I close my eyes and think about that specific kiss, it's like fireworks on the Fourth of July going off in my head. He just made me so happy.

A short while later, we were in his car driving down to the beach to watch the sunset. The drive was calming. It was a feeling that I hadn't felt in a long time; being in a moment where everything was still and perfect. Our hands were intertwined, fitting perfectly inside one another's the entire way. Every now and then, Dalton would turn to look at me and just smile. We didn't say much during that drive. There wasn't really much *to* say. There was more of a feeling of being safe and being loved that fueled the lack of conversation between the two of us; like we knew we were meant to be. We could have stayed in that drive forever—forever feeling our hearts connected with our unspoken words. I kind of wish I was there now. Every now and then, he would squeeze my hand and slowly bring it up to his lips, giving it the gentlest little kiss. I can still feel his hand in mine, and that makes my heart happy.

When we finally got to the beach, Dalton pulled a blanket out of his trunk, along with a bottle of Champagne. How was he that amazing? He was so kind and thoughtful, and I was so, very much in love with him.

We lay on the beach far beyond the sun setting, breaking our silence to talk about our childhoods and about our dreams for the future.

"So, why acting?" he asked.

"I've always loved movies and being on stage. Performing, really. It was kind of a way for me to escape when I was growing up."

"Escape from what?"

"Well, I don't usually like to tell people, but my parents died in a car accident when I was eight, so my grandmother raised me. She's the one that got me into old Hollywood films. We did everything together, and she never treated me weird like everybody else did, which I loved. God, you would have loved her, she was so funny. She would get a huge kick out of Chad and Sebastian, that's for sure, and she would be happy that I have Roxy as a friend. And she would definitely be shocked at the life I'm living now, that I'm actually out here pursuing my dreams."

"Yeah, and what would she think about me?" he asked.

It was hard to come up with just the right words to say to him without revealing how my heart felt, so I was honest in a way. "Oh, she'd love you."

"Yeah?"

"Oh, yeah! She'd think you were very handsome, smart, charming... She'd be very happy that you were in my life."

"So where is she now? Back home?"

"No, she passed about a year before I moved out here."

"I'm sorry, Julie."

"Oh, don't be. It's okay." I smiled. "But, please don't tell the others. I don't want them to be awkward around me."

"I won't, I promise," he said and smiled at me as I turned towards him. "Well, I'm glad that I would make her happy. I think that I'd love her too."

"Yeah, she always made me feel so special and very much loved. So, when I moved out here, I decided that I just wouldn't say anything to anyone. I didn't want them to feel sorry for me. I got those looks a lot as a kid and it always bothered me, so if anyone asked me about my family, I would just say that they still lived back in Missouri," I explained.

"I get it. I kind of had a similar upbringing."

"Really?" I questioned. "How so?"

"Well, my mom wasn't really a mom. She cared more about the party and getting fucked up than she did about me. So, my nannies were the mother figures in my life. But my mom always found a problem with one of them, so they never stuck around more than a few months to a year. Genevieve was my favorite though. She stayed with me for two years before she finally had enough of my mom's shit. She would have been gone a lot sooner, but she actually cared about me, which was really nice. She put up with my mom for as long as she did for my best interests. But when I was 16, my mom was done with me and bought me my own house. I mean, she loves me, don't get me wrong. Her way of thinking that she's a good Mother is buying me things and letting me do whatever I want. Which don't get me wrong, had its perks," he laughed. "But growing up, all I ever wanted was just a hug from her or for her to tell me that she loved me."

Our lives were different, but one in the same. We didn't have our parents. Although we were loved and had happy lives, there was still always something missing, and there was always a pity taken upon us.

The evening was perfect, and I learned much more than I ever had expected to about Dalton Blake. I felt very lucky.

"I've always had a passion for writing and for music."

"Really? What have you written?"

"Just a few songs here and there," he said, shrugging and looking out into the distance.

"Do you play anything? Or sing?" I asked with a growing smile on my face.

"No, I just write the lyrics," he paused. "Poems, really."

"Can I read one?" I gazed lovingly at him.

"Maybe on our fourth date," he smiled at me. "We're halfway there," he said, and began tickling me until I fell backwards in the sand with him landing on top of me. "You're so beautiful Julie," he said, looking deeply into my eyes, like he was actually looking at *me*. He slowly brought his face closer, without ever taking his eyes from mine, and passionately started to kiss me, brushing his hand against my face and gently caressing down to my chest and over my breast until his fingertips were the only things touching me. One by one, they disappeared until his hand braised my lower back and he pulled me in.

We stayed at the beach for a few hours, not really keeping track of time, and not caring about our lives back in Beverly Hills. In those few hours, we were just two people getting to know one another and starting to share the same feelings towards each other. We were ordinary people. Just a boy and a girl, falling in love.

"Yeah, I do love acting and it's my dream to get a

leading role, but I would really love to have a family. I want to have little babies and love them how my parents loved me. I guess I mostly want what I really didn't have. So, I'm going to make it for myself. I'll be there helping my daughter when she's getting ready on her wedding day, and I'll be there, teaching my son how to really treat a girl. I'll be there when they have their hearts broken for the first time. It's lame, I know but..."

"It's not lame at all. You're going to be the best Mom, Julie. You know," he paused. "I never really thought about all of that before, but hearing you talk about it makes me want it too."

I smiled, knowing in my heart that he was telling me the truth.

"I've never met anyone like you before, Julie."

"Oh, come on! You must have, you're Dalton Blake," I said back, playfully pushing his arm.

"No, I'm serious," he said. "I know a lot of people and I've been around a lot of people, but I've never met anyone that has a heart like yours..."

That heart that he was talking about began racing, but also slowing to a calmness. He was perfectly playing at my heartstrings.

"You're so beautiful, Julie."

"Yeah, I think you said that already," I smiled, blushing.

"No, I mean it. Julie, you are the most beautiful woman I've ever seen. I... you just make me feel so good. You make me want things that I've never wanted before, the life you talked about. You make me want... you," he said, with a tender look in his eyes. Then he just kept looking at me, like he wanted to tell me something or like he wanted to say more. Instead, he brushed the side of my face and kissed me again.

On the drive home I asked him a question that had been nagging at me. "Hey, why aren't you talking to Roxy right now?

He answered plainly, "She did something that I really didn't like." He seemed to get a little tense.

I left it at that.

But that drive back to Roxy's seemed too quick. I didn't want my night with Dalton to ever end. I wanted to be with him forever.

When we got to the door, I stopped and turned towards him. "Do you have to go?"

"I'm not going anywhere."

We laid in bed and started to watch a movie. We had had the best night. This was the side of Dalton Blake that I was the only person in the whole world to know about and get to see. He was so gentle and caring, and he wanted more in life than cars and a trust fund. And when he looked into my eyes, it was as if he were reading my soul, word for word, and taking in their true meaning. He was my soulmate, and I was madly in love with him.

"I wish that we could stay like this forever," I said as I lay there wrapped in his arms, knowing that that was exactly where I was supposed to be. With my head gently laying on his chest, the sound of his beating heart was the lullaby drifting me off to sleep.

"Me too," he said softly, as he lightly gave me a kiss on the top of my head. Just as my eyes were falling heavy, he whispered, "I'm sorry, Julie. I should have protected you."

And just like that, I was left to my dreams.

Chapter Eleven

Two more days passed before I decided that I would go back home to my apartment— back to the damage of my life that I was trying to move on from. I hesitated at the door, not wanting to see the mess that awaited me and have terrible memories flood back into my mind. So I stood there, taking deep breaths until I was ready. Finally, I turned the key slowly and pushed the door open. I stood there, not able to believe what was before my eyes. Everything was clean and back to how it was before that terrifying night. I stood there confused, thinking about what had taken place over such a short period of time, and it baffled me. There I was, standing in what had been a room of utter dismay just a few days prior, but it was now just the way I had left it. My safe place. Just like the last time I had locked my door before that night.

"Hey Roxy! I just wanted to say thank you for the

past couple of days. And thanks for sending someone to clean my apartment."

"Don't thank me, thank Dalton," she said, as she quickly hung up the phone.

Dalton? Dalton was the one who sent someone to clean up my nightmare? It was so sweet of him. He never seemed to miss a beat when it came to me. He always knew what to say or do. He always knew how to make me love him even more.

My heart felt full again, almost as if I wasn't as lonely anymore. I had people. I had friends. Friends that cared about me. Friends that had pushed the boundaries of me as a person, and nearly ended my life, but they did it out of a wanting for me. And I had him. It was a good feeling. Los Angeles wasn't this big land of the unknown anymore—it was home. It was my new home, with my new family.

I went to work that night trying to get back to somewhat of a normal life. Fortunately, Jeffery and Dawson had the night off. I couldn't bear to have them see me and ask what I had been up to. I was ashamed that I had just left them behind, but I was in a good place with good people, and nothing or no one would change that.

After work, I decided that I would bring Dalton a bottle of nice champagne to thank him for having my apartment cleaned up. I took a quick shower and got dressed into something cute; something that I thought he would like. Something that was *me*.

At 11 p.m., I headed over to Dalton's. His car was in the

driveway, so I knew that he was home. I knocked on his front door and waited a minute. My nerves were welling up inside. No answer. I tried the doorbell. My heart was pounding, endlessly. No answer, so I knocked one last time. When there was again no answer, I figured that Dalton either didn't hear it or didn't want to answer because he didn't know who was at the door. I knew that I should have called, but I wanted to surprise him. The last time that Roxy and I had come over, we just walked in, so I decided to try that. I turned the handle and, to my luck, it was unlocked.

I opened the door slowly. "Dalton?"

No answer.

I continued into his house. "Dalton? It's Jules. I mean, Julie. Are you home?"

Nothing.

His house was very him—the him that I knew alone, not with Roxy and the guys. I hadn't noticed it before, but it was elegant for a 24-year-old guy, with paintings that were so beautiful, they looked like masterpieces. They could have been the real thing. With my upbringing, who knew, maybe they were. He even had a little corner with a grand piano and a few guitars. That was probably where he wrote his songs.

The mansion was dark. I began to walk in slowly to search for him. With every twist and turn, there was a mystery, just like Dalton. Everything from the dining room table to the gold candle fixtures on the mantle that were so luxurious, they could have belonged to the Royal Family. But why were they there, and did he pick them out? His Mom was probably the one who decorated it, and if she did, she knew her son without really knowing him. She knew about his gentle soul, about the way he cared for people under his dark demeanor. She knew about his rugged touch that you feared yet craved at the same time. About how, no matter how hard you tried to concentrate on something else, the craving for him set in and began to flow through your veins. You lived for him. It sounds silly, but Dalton was special, and he knew it. I mean, he was Dalton Blake.

I was yearning for him at that point. Yearning for his touch, his gaze, his lips upon mine. That tingling feeling you get when you want something so bad it makes your toes curl. Just the lust of hoping that he would be so happy to see me, that I would run into those arms that I wanted wrapped around me so badly. Needing them to caress my every curve and every imperfection. Needing that feeling of being loved and satisfied. Just needing him.

Dalton Blake was like the greatest drug out there. Once you had a little taste, you wanted more. You needed more. There was a pining for him; an undeniable attraction to everything about him. And no matter how hard you tried to push him out of your mind, your heart, body, and soul were feigning for him. You wanted him to take over every part of you; for him to attach himself to you and destroy you without there being a way for him to get out of you. He made you feel like you were on a never-ending high when you had him. And when you didn't, you would do anything to get that feeling back—to get him back. He just gave you this *rush*.

Room by room, I went searching, roused with the

feeling that he was there. Somewhere, behind one of these walls, he was playing a little game of hide and seek with me. Every time I peeked around a corner, my heart would race with so much intensity, ecstatic that I could possibly see him. And when he would spot me, he'd be so happy that I was there. We'd wrap our arms around each other and never let go. I was also thinking that when I did find him, who knew what would happen. At this point, anything was possible.

I searched until there was one room left—his room.

For someone who made me feel so comfortable and safe, he still made those butterflies flutter like their lives depended on it.

Breathe. I had to remind myself to breathe.

There was no answer when I knocked.

"Dalton?"

No answer.

I slowly began to turn the handle and open his door.

Then I saw it.

Chapter Twelve

I couldn't move. As I stood there, frozen in place, my body started shaking. I couldn't believe what I was seeing; what was right in front of me. The guy that I was in love with, who I thought cared about me, who I had opened up to and was prepared to give all of myself to, was in bed with my friend. My best friend.

A million things were running through my mind in the seconds that I stood there, shocked. *Who in the hell did she think she was? I mean, I thought that Roxy only dated older guys and she knew that I loved him, right? Is she even really my best friend? Do people out here do this kind of stuff and think that it's okay? Who in the hell were these people?*

"Hey, Jules," he said in a hurried and nervous tone, as if nothing was going on, but also knowing that he got caught.

Roxy had this look on her face like she was mad that I

interrupted, but also like she was having fun with it at the same time.

As soon as I was able to move, I dropped the bottle of champagne and ran. I didn't know what else to do. My heart was broken—it had shattered into a million pieces along with the bottle. I was betrayed by my best friend and by the guy that I was in love with, and they both knew it.

Dalton began to chase after me, calling out my name. "Julie! Julie! Wait!"

It must have been my imagination. My world began swirling around me and I could barely see through the tears welling up in my eyes. I was running what felt like a marathon, running faster than I had ever run before. My head and my legs lost sight of one another, and I tripped down a few stairs, but was able to scramble to my feet and continue to get out of there.

He didn't reach me; he wasn't even close. By the time he got out of the door, I was already out of his driveway.

I was done with them. I was done with Los Angeles, and I was done with my dream. I would move back home once I could think clearly. This just wasn't what I thought it would be. It wasn't the life I wanted to live—at least not anymore.

At work, I stopped avoiding Jeffery and Dawson, and like the true gentle, caring, loving guys that they were, they embraced me back with open arms.

"Julie, we've been worried about you," Dawson said. "Where have you been?"

"I tried calling you so many times over the past few

weeks, I was so worried that something had happened to you," Jeffery said.

If only they knew.

"I know, I know, I've been such a bitch and an awful friend to the two of you. I just kind of got wrapped up in the whole Beverly Hills shindig." I paused. "But that's all over now and I'm so sorry guys. I love you, and I hope that you can forgive me and still love me too."

"Of course, Julie, what are friends for?" Jeffery embraced me in a warm hug.

I didn't tell them any of the bizarre instances that had happened to me since I had been in the land of the "cool kids." They asked if I wanted to talk about it all, but I couldn't tell them. Everything that had happened up until that point didn't seem real. If you really look at it, it doesn't seem like any of that could ever happen to just one person, right? And who knew what they would think or want to do. I just wanted to forget it all, but it was easier said than done. I kept to myself for a day or two trying to wrap my head around all of the thoughts moving through my mind, and all of the pain that was in my heart. It's one thing if a guy wants to be with someone while leading another girl on, but why would someone who says that they're my best friend completely betray me? That was my big question. My mind wouldn't stop replaying the last few weeks over and over in my head, while my heart wouldn't stop reliving a few days ago. Everything felt like it was falling apart. My career, my social life. Me.

Although every bad thing felt unreal, the worst part

was that I missed them. I actually *missed* them. Even Sebastian. And especially Roxy, my best friend. And him. Dalton Blake. I missed him so much; I missed everything about him.

After a long shift, I got home ready to crash, but saw that I had a message on my machine. By then I hadn't heard from them for about a week, so I didn't consider that it would be from one of them. I just figured that it was Dawson, who wasn't at work, seeing if I wanted to go out.

"You have 10 new messages," the automated voice informed me.

No one ever really called me. No one ever really left a message. I didn't have any family and I now only talked to two people—my original friends in LA—so I was stunned to hear that I had so many messages.

"Hey Jules, it's me! I'm so sorry for the other night. That was a big misunderstanding and I..."

Delete.

The sound of her voice sent chills up and down my spine. I didn't even want to listen to the rest of the messages, I just deleted them all. What could she possibly say to explain the long knife of betrayal that she stabbed me in the back with?

My emotions went from disgust, to anger, to rage, to sadness, and then pure hatred, and I wasn't raised to feel that way towards someone. My Grandmother taught me to love all people, no matter how much of a snake they were. Treat them how I would want to be treated. But again, it was easier said than done when I had been hurt in so many ways from the delusional people that I wanted so badly to be my friends.

I took a bubble bath to relax and decided to sit by my window and read a book to escape my current reality. As I sat there, I looked out and saw my favorite trees—my palm trees. They looked so elegant, like no one could ever hurt them or would even want to. They just stood there, so regal, as if they were there watching over me. I know that they aren't the strongest of trees, but to me, they were my protectors. I always got lost in them. Every ridge and detail of their long trunks fascinated me. The beautiful green fronds made them seem like my favorite old Hollywood starlets, wearing their headpieces during their dance numbers. I could just look at them, for hours, and feel that I was safe; that I was with someone or something familiar. That I wasn't alone. I would miss seeing them every day when I would eventually be back home. But at that moment, I knew the only way that I was going to get on with my life was to put these people as far away from me as possible.

At work the following day, I was starting to feel better knowing that I was disassociating myself from the Beverly Hills "in crowd." Work was work as usual, customers coming in and out, just like another ordinary day. The hostess told me that I had a new table, so I went to greet them and to get their drink order. I nearly froze when I saw who was sitting at the table. It was her. Roxy.

My heart was fuming with anger, and I didn't want to approach. I was about to walk away when I saw my manager at the next table.

"Hi, I'm Julie, I'll be your waitress today. Can I start you off with a drink?" I said, pretending that I didn't know her.

"Jules, I didn't know how else to talk to you. I tried calling, but you never returned my messages," she began.

Pretend that you don't know her. Pretend that you don't know her, I repeated in my head.

"We have a great Mai Tai and a delicious strawberry lemonade," I smiled.

"Jules, I'm sorry. I..."

I couldn't handle it. I walked away fast and angry.

Jeffery was in the kitchen, and I asked him to cover my table. Once out of sight, I ran out back, hyperventilating. My breath wouldn't catch up to my lungs. I felt like the ground was spinning and I was about to faint. It must have been ten minutes that had passed when I felt well enough to go back inside.

"She left," Jeffery said.

"Thank God." Relief fell over me.

"She left this for you though," Jeffery said, handing me a napkin.

Slowly, I opened the neatly folded napkin. *'You know you're still one of us,'* was written across it.

Tears began pouring down my face. This cryptic message meant nothing, yet everything to me. But *what* did it mean?

I crumpled up the napkin and threw it away. I threw

it all away: my morals, my dignity, my compassion, my life.

There was a message waiting for me when I got home. "Jules!!!!! It's Sebastian, wanna come play?"

Delete.

The following day when I got home from work, there was yet another message left for me. "Jules, I thought that you wanted to be one of us?" Chad's voice said over the speaker. Delete.

After a week and a half of harassing voicemails, I was about ready to give up. I started to feel sick from all of the stress. I was dizzy. I was nauseous almost all day long, and then I began vomiting every morning for three days straight.

I decided that I would go and see a doctor in hopes that they could prescribe me something for the continuous, anxious feeling of my heart wanting to beat straight out of my chest.

"How long have you been sick?" Dr. Haggerty asked.

"I guess about a week and a half now. I've been really stressed out, so I'm thinking that it came from that. But I've also been vomiting for the past few mornings."

"Have you had any unprotected sex lately?" he asked.

"No, I've never had sex, I'm a..." I froze. What was I supposed to say to the doctor? It was embarrassing and shameful to admit something so horrible to a complete stranger. As much as I didn't want to believe it, I had to finally admit it. "Well, about a month ago I was—" I could barely get the word out of my mouth. "—raped," I whispered.

He looked at me. He was sorry for me, I could tell. I didn't want people to look at me like that. I was looked at like that practically my entire life. But he had an added look of sadness, and also wonder, as to how I could let something like that happen to me.

"And did you go to the hospital afterwards to get checked out?" he asked as sincerely as he could.

"No, I wasn't quite sure if I even really was ra..." I paused. "So, my friend told me that I didn't have to get checked out."

"Julie, in cases like that you have to go and get yourself checked out. You have to see if there's any DNA so that the police can trace it, and try to get the person who did this to you off of the streets." He paused and looked at me. "I know that it can be scary, but it's really important that you report it, even now that some time has passed," he continued.

Dr. Haggerty gave me a blood test, a urine test, and examined me in full to see if there was anything else wrong with me besides stress and anxiety.

I waited 30 minutes—the longest 30 minutes.

When he walked back into the room, he had a wary look on his face.

"Is everything okay? Did you find something?" I asked, worried.

He sat down on a stool in front of me and placed his hand gently on my knee. "Julie, I'm afraid that I did find something," he began. "Julie, you are," he paused again before finishing, "pregnant."

I began crying uncontrollably. I was mad; mad at myself. I should have just gone to the police. I was so stupid. Why was I so dense as to let some girl have control over my own actions? Who cares if it could ruin her dad's career, it was now ruining *my* life.

Tears were pouring down my face, my mind full of anger and my heart full of shame. There was now a life *inside* of me. How could I bring another person into this world when I could barely handle living in it myself?

Dr. Haggerty stood up and began to hug me.

I leaned into his hug, letting my body fall, and I whispered, "That was my first time."

I left the doctor's office in a trance. There were people moving around me; happy people, going about their normal everyday lives. But I didn't see any of them. They were all a blur. And I didn't want to let a stranger see me cry. I didn't want them to wonder what was wrong with me, or with *us*. I had experienced that my entire childhood. I needed to be brave and figure this out. I had to plan what the rest of my life would look like. Whether it was just going to be me, or me and a child.

When I got into the hallway of my apartment, Roxy was waiting at my door. I shoved her aside to put the key in the lock. I was pissed that she was there and that she had the audacity to come to my home and bombard me like that. I was pissed that she was the one who ruined my life. If only I had gone to the police, then maybe things would be different. But I was mostly pissed because she was the *one* person that I wanted to tell everything to. I couldn't take it anymore; it was too much to hold in. I broke down and fell to the floor. She must have seen how much pain I was in, and to my surprise, she bent down and held me.

Through my cry, I managed to say, "I'm pregnant."

Her eyes widened. "We'll get through this, Jules. We'll get it taken care of." She started rocking me in a slow motion, holding me close. "I'll help you, Jules, I'm here."

She then helped me get up and into bed. "I'm going to come over tomorrow morning and take you to a clinic, okay? Get some rest tonight, and tomorrow it will all be over with." She gently brushed her hand over my hair and left.

I fell into a long, hard sleep.

I woke up to pounding on my door. It must have been at least 10 o'clock, because the sun was shining and the birds were chirping. I didn't want to get out of bed. I just wanted to throw the covers over my head and fall back to sleep to escape my reality.

"Jules, it's me! Open up!" she yelled as I was about to turn the doorknob. "You look like hell," she said. "Get dressed. We have an 11:30 appointment, so hurry up."

I don't remember getting dressed. I just remember that I was staring blankly at the palm trees the entire way to the clinic, wishing that I could be one of them so that no one could hurt me anymore.

We walked into a small, dark office after a long, quiet drive. I mean, what could I even say? I was in a position that I never thought I would ever find myself in, in a city that I still wasn't even sure of. I sat down and let Roxy do all of the talking. The only thing that I did was walk into the small room and lay there with my eyes closed, tears gently rolling down my cheeks until the procedure was over. That's all I could do. I was numb.

When we got back to my apartment, Roxy put me in bed, and I fell back into my escape. I fell back into my dreams.

Chapter Thirteen

Four days had passed when I was finally able to get out of bed. The phone was ringing, and although I didn't want to talk to anyone, I still picked up.

"Jules, it's Roxy. We're all at Dalton's hanging out. You should come."

"No, thank you." I hung up.

The phone immediately began ringing again.

"Hello?" I answered angrily.

"Jules, you better come over," she said, her tone hateful.

As much as I didn't want to, because of the agony that I had gone through since meeting this girl, I decided that I should probably go and get back to some version of my normal life, whatever that was. I guess I wasn't done with them.

Dalton's house seemed messy when I walked in; things were out of place and it smelled disgusting. I walked into the living room and saw Chad and Sebastian sitting down, smoking what reminded me of skunk, but I didn't care. In that second if they offered, I would have taken whatever they had. I just didn't want to be anywhere anymore. I needed a stronger escape.

"Hey Jules, how are you feeling?" Chad asked.

I didn't answer. I just flopped down into a chair and stared out the window. That's when Dalton walked in.

He walked right up to me and tried to give me a kiss. I turned my head the other way. Why would I want those filthy lips on me now? Did he not remember what happened the last time I was over there and found him in bed with my best friend? It was like it didn't faze him.

"Jules, come here. I need you to help me pick out an outfit," Roxy demanded.

I just glared at her like I could care less, because I really couldn't. I kept thinking to myself, *Why in the hell did I even come here? Why in the hell do I keep doing this to myself?*

Walking down that hallway brought up the worst memories. All I could think about was the image of the two people I cared about most, naked and intertwined with one another. And of me, standing there speechless and stupid, unable to move from the doorway, like a complete fool.

We got inside of Dalton's room and Roxy's things were strewn all over the place, more so than the last time I saw them like this.

"Why are your clothes in Dalton's room?" I asked.

"I live here now," she replied nonchalantly.

That *fucking* bitch!

Rage began to come over me as I stood in front of the one person that I now truly hated, my so-called "Best Friend." I had to keep my cool while I figured out what was going on, and why all of a sudden, everything in my life had done a 180 and was punching me back in the face.

"Hey, Roxy, have you mentioned anything to your father about possibly getting me an audition? I know that you said that you would, but I was just curious if you had said anything yet?"

No answer.

In her usual selfish fashion, she ignored me and proceeded to walk out of the closet in her now-changed outfit. "Does this look cute enough to hang out in?"

Really? Just play it cool, Jules.

"Yes, but Roxy, have you mentioned getting me an audition to your father yet?"

Ignored again. This girl who I had once revered as the most beautiful girl I had ever seen and could not believe that she would even hang out with me, let alone talk to me, was now undoubtedly the worst person I had ever come across. She was hideous and evil, inside and out. I guess sometimes the worst people come with the most beautiful faces.

I tried to keep calm. I tried to bite my tongue, but everything that had been building up for the past few months had finally come to its tipping point.

"Do you even care about anyone besides yourself?" I snapped.

That got her attention.

"Oh, so little miss goodie two shoes wants to come out and play, huh?" she said, her tone evil; sinister even. "Just because we took pity on your poor, pathetic, little life and let you hang out with us, you think that we owe you?" She paused. "Well, we don't. You are a nobody! No one will ever know who you are, because you're just some sad, desperate, small-town little girl who is forgettable." She started to slowly walk towards me. "You walk around here like you're the shit because you think that we're your friends, but let me tell you something, Jules, we aren't! And let me tell you something else! Your beloved Dalton, who you are so cutely, schoolgirl in love with, never liked you. He never wanted to even talk to you, but I made him."

What was going on? Dalton? There was no way. She was jealous. She had to be. I was so confused, but that had to be it. By that time, she had backed me into the corner of the room and kept belittling me, to the point where I started to panic and thoughts of fearing for my life began to settle in. I still didn't know who she really was. I'd never seen this side of her. This was the mean, bitchy, side Chad and Sebastian had talked about. Sure, it was possible to know someone in just a few short months, but it was now clear to me that she definitely wasn't one of those kinds of people.

"He told me when he took you on your little 'night on the town,' but honey I planned it all. I made him do it, and I told him everywhere that he should take you; a drive down Rodeo, a little one-on-one look at the stars at the Griffith Observatory, and especially The Chateau

Marmont. He hates that place. He says that it's full of washed-up stars trying to go back to their hay day, but I knew that that place would sucker you in. And that kiss. That moment you thought was so magical. I told him to do it. He didn't want to." She smirked, glaring at me with sinister eyes. "You're so pathetic. Some might even say weak. Yeah, you're just a little weak wannabe that thought she was a hot little something for a while, but is now realizing that she's scum. A piece of trash," she paused. "An *orphan*."

He told her. He promised that he wouldn't, and I believed him. I was even more angry and baffled then, but I didn't want to correct her while she was in such a fit of rage. Tears kept streaming down my red, fuming cheeks, and my heart was pounding with anger.

"Oh, so you're gonna cry now? Typical little Julie Simon. *I'm so sad and perfect. I don't ever do anything bad.* Yeah, right! Don't think for one second that I haven't been watching you, Jules. You were the one throwing yourself on guys at The Viper Room. You were asking for it."

The door swung open. I was hoping that it was going to be Dalton coming to save me from Roxy, who had suddenly flipped a switch and gone crazy, but my hopes were shattered.

"Well, what do we have here? A little fight?" Chad asked.

"A chick fight? Are ya gonna roll around naked on the floor?" Sebastian added.

"I'm just putting her in her place," she glared with a

face full of evil. "She thinks that we're actually her friends." Roxy laughed.

"Well, friend, why did you have to go and kill my baby?" Chad asked. "And by the way, I enjoyed being your first. Personally, it was a little messy. I'm not a fan of blood," he said, looking at Sebastian. "But you were lousy, Jules. If you want, I can teach you. You know, show you some things."

My heart was racing as I stood there, terrified. Who were these people? Were they that bored with their lives that they had turned to playing someone a fool?

"Hey Jules, I've been meaning to tell you, nice panty drawer. I'm not really into the granny panty styles but—" Sebastian said. "Oh, Rox, when we were there, she had written Mrs. Dalton Blake all over some piece of paper by her answering machine," he continued, laughing.

"Oh my God, what a loser." She laughed again.

I was struggling to get out of the barrier they had made around me. I was sobbing and shaking uncontrollably with fear. I didn't know what they would do next, or what they could even do at all. I just wanted to get home and to get away from these psychotic people that were in front of me. People that I had blindly let into my life.

Finally, somehow, I managed to kick Sebastian in the shin and was able to spring out of the small space that opened up when he jumped back.

Running down the hall, I bumped into Dalton. "You're all crazy," I screamed through my tears. "Who do you think you are? How can you all do this to someone?"

Dalton grabbed me and hugged me tightly. "Julie,

don't listen to them. They just wanted to have a little fun and—"

"Fun? You call this fun? What the hell, Dalton?!" I was trying to pull away, but his grip around me was tight. I kept trying to wiggle free, but he kept bringing me in even closer and then he kissed me.

I pulled away from him. "Let me go!" I said sternly, my teeth clenched. He kept trying to grab me, wanting me to be near him. I wanted to surrender myself into the arms that made me feel safe, but I couldn't. I pushed him away again, looking into his eyes as I yelled, "Dalton, you are the worst one of them all. I saw you with her. It was all a lie, she told me..." I started to cry once more.

"Julie, don't listen to Roxy, it's real." He pulled me in close to him. "She's the crazy one here. Trust me." He looked at me deeply. "Julie..."

"If it's so real, then why won't you help me?"

"Julie, I... I lo..."

Just then, Roxy and the guys came out of the room.

"Oh, Jules, how come you don't want to play with us anymore?" Sebastian asked in a childlike voice.

I loosened from Dalton's grip and ran as fast as I could to my car, never looking back.

At home I was safe. The door was locked as soon as I ran through it. I even stuck a chair under the knob just in case. I jumped into bed sobbing, covering myself with my blankets, thinking about how unlucky I was to have ever met those people. I was too into the idea of being one of them that I looked past all of the warning signs that urged me to stay away. I felt so stupid. I was disappointed in myself.

But what I still couldn't wrap my mind around was how people could be like them. How manipulative, yet alluring, they could be. And how I could even still be thinking about them and wanting their acceptance. I had lost myself and who I was, and I needed to get her back. I needed to be strong. I needed to leave this place—like, actually leave this time—and never look back.

As I began drifting off to sleep, I could see the palm trees outside of my window, and I felt safe; like everything was going to be okay.

Chapter Fourteen

The only reason that I knew it was 3 a.m. was because I had just gotten back into bed after getting a glass of water. The phone rang.

"Meet me at Runyon Canyon off of Mulholland Drive," she said quickly.

I hung up.

Just as I was drifting back off to sleep, the phone started ringing again. "Stop calling me, Roxy. I never wanna talk to you ever aga—"

"Julie." His voice. It still got me. He could still somehow stop me in my tracks and make me forget about everything that they had done to me—everything *he* had done to me. That's why he was the worst one; he was infectious. He hurt me the most, because he hurt my heart, and even though it was completely broken, I was still so in love with him that if he asked me to forget about everything and run away with him, I would in a heart-beat. What got me the most were those slow vibrations in his voice that made every nerve tingle with the sensitivity of a feather, lightly drifting up and down my thigh. It's that good feeling that you know is bad. It was something that you wanted to happen and didn't want to happen at the same time, just because of who he was.

There was silence.

It was all a lie. She knew that I couldn't say no to Dalton. To this perfect, yet unperfect man that I was so in love with, even though he didn't love me back. Someone who really loved me wouldn't hurt me so badly. She just knew I couldn't say no.

"Being with Roxy was a mistake. I've always had a thing for you, Julie. You know that," he said coolly. "You're my girl, remember?"

I did know that. I think that I always did. No, it couldn't be. "If you've always had a thing for me, then why didn't you help me when they were terrorizing me in your own home, Dalton? Or save me when I was drowning? Or protect me from getting raped?" I paused for a second to see if he would respond. He didn't so I continued. "And why does Roxy live at your house? In your room!" There were so many questions to be answered— too many questions—and no answers. "You said not to listen to her, and that it's real, but what does that even mean? You should be taking your own advice, Dalton." I paused, again. As a few teardrops slowly slid down my cheeks, I asked, "What more do you want from me?"

Silence.

"Julie," his voice cracked. "Please come."

What could I say? Everything was telling me to not

go, not to give in to their peer pressure again. I just couldn't fully wrap my head around what made me need their approval so badly. Why should *I* go and put myself in quite possibly *another* dangerous situation where I would be left to pick up my own shattered pieces? And then it would hit me again, like a gigantic wave crashing over me. Because of him. *He* still had me. He always would.

"Fine. I'll be there soon."

"We'll be waiting. And Julie," he paused. "I lo..."

I hung up before he could finish, and dragged myself out of bed. I got dressed and started to drive to them, thinking to myself how idiotic I was. I could have turned back at any point; I should have turned back. But during that drive, I kept trying to come up with what I would say to them—to *her*—so that I could stand my ground and control the situation.

As I was approaching, the drive up the dark, unlit road made me start to feel uneasy and worried. What were they doing up here in the middle of the night, exactly? And why did they need *me* to come?

My eyes were immediately drawn to Dalton, who was pacing back and forth, muttering to himself. It was odd behavior, and not how he normally acted or seemed to carry himself. It was almost as if he were in shock or a panic. My heart fell to my stomach, sending warning signals to my brain, but it wasn't deciphering what was going on. I heard a little rustle and turned my head to see Roxy sitting on the ground, with her head on her knees, and her arms wrapped around her legs, tightly. She was crying. And again, my brain wasn't registering what the pit in my stomach was trying to tell me; it was listening to my heart and the love that I had for these two people. The two people that meant both nothing and everything to me.

"What are you guys doing?" I asked, getting out of my car. I started to walk over to Dalton. "Dalton, what's going on? Are you guys, okay?" I asked, alarmed.

When he finally stopped pacing, I had gotten closer to him—almost within arm's reach. He turned towards me, and I noticed his eyes had turned dark; like the man that I loved no longer existed. It was frightening. He looked hollow, like he lost whatever it was that made him seem so tough and masculine; what made him *him*. That's when I knew, for certain, that something wasn't right. My brain finally started to receive those warning calls, but I didn't know what to do. It felt too late.

"Dalton?" I said, slowly reaching my hand out to touch him.

"Julie. No, Julie. Julie, Julie, Julie," he rambled, in a cry of panic and fear. "Julie, no," he cried harder. "Julie, you shouldn't have come. She... you shouldn't have come!"

"Come on Dalton, it's okay. Take my hand and we can go. I'll take you out of here. We can go home," I said, putting my other arm up towards his shoulder.

"It wasn't supposed to be like this," he hyperventilated between cries. "I wasn't supposed to, but I fell Julie, I fell for yo... It shouldn't be you."

"What are you talking about?"

Just then he looked past me, and his eyes widened like something was approaching. "NO! DON'T!" He yelled with such a force that as I began to turn around, an overwhelming sense of fear began to rise up in my chest...

BANG.

Everything went dark.

When I opened my eyes, the back of my head had an immense pain, and I could feel a wetness when I reached up to touch it. The pain was coursing through my entire body, and I could barely move. I was scared. Slowly, I moved my head up and around. Roxy wasn't crouched down crying anymore, and Dalton wasn't there in front of me. I was alone; they were nowhere in sight. The darkness of the night made it hard to see even a few feet in front of me, but I knew with everything in me that I had to get out of there, and I had to get out of there fast.

Standing was nearly impossible for the radiating pain in my brain. Crawling seemed to be the only option for my own safety; I didn't want to fall. As I began to put my hands in front of me and slowly pull myself through the dry dirt and brush, I felt a familiar feeling. It was soft, yet sturdy, and it was cold. Wearily, I put my hands out even further to feel what it could be. It was long and hard, and wet in one area. Flesh. Human flesh.

Frightened, I tried to scramble as far away as my pain ridden body would allow. My heart immediately sank once more, thinking that the flesh that I had felt was Dalton—my Dalton. But why? And who?

"What the hell, Roxy? This isn't funny anymore!" My voice quivered. "Where are you?" No answers. I looked towards the body in front of me, and with tears starting to run down my cheeks, I asked the one thing that I didn't want to be true. "Dalton?"

Once again, no answers. "What's going on?" I began sobbing. "Roxy? Dalton? Why is this happening to me? Where are you? Answer me!" I screamed.

As I tried to tussle around to see any sort of sign or indication that I too hadn't been left for dead, I heard sirens, and they were rapidly approaching. Why was I here? What was happening? He said that it shouldn't be me, what did that mean? What were the police going to find when they got here? When they found *me*?

Panic. The all too familiar feeling I had been experiencing for months hit me harder and faster than it had before. I had to run, but the blow to my head made it so hard to get up. I stumbled as I began to move my feet in front of me, not knowing where I was running to. The darkness and the throbbing in my head impaired my vision, not letting my eyes adjust. But then I saw it. The dark, statuesque and eminent outline of my palm trees. I stopped in my tracks, and was suddenly overcome by a feeling of knowing that somehow, everything would be okay. *I* would be okay.

Chapter Fifteen

"Why did you do it, Miss Simon?"

"I didn't do it," I pleaded. "I told you already, Roxy Harrington and Dalton Blake have been harassing me for *months*. They were the ones who almost drowned me, drugged me, got me raped, and called me to meet them there tonight."

"We don't have any attempted drownings or rapes filed in a police report, Miss Simon. How do we even know you're telling us the truth?" Detective Johnson asked.

"You *have* to believe me," I pleaded, again. "These are *not* nice people. They manipulate everyone they meet. Trust me," I cried. "No one wants to be their friend; they don't even want to be near them. People hate them, they fear them."

"You didn't," the detective said.

She had me there. I didn't fear them. They were my

friends and I cared for them deeply, even after all of the torturous things they had done to me. Hate them, yes. But to fear them? I couldn't.

"I thought that Roxy *was* my friend. I met her when I was auditioning for her dad..."

"Richard Harrington? The director?" Detective Johnson asked.

"Yes. I didn't have a good audition, and when she saw me crying, she must have known that I was weak, that I would be easy to manipulate."

"Into killing someone?" the detective asked.

"Yes. I mean, no. That must be how they get their kicks in life. They do things to people that hurt them, and they *know* that they can get away with it. You have to believe me. Please! They have money and that gives them power. Can't you see that?"

"It just doesn't make sense, Miss Simon. Why would they get off on something like that? They didn't have a motive," she pressured. "But you did."

I was completely bewildered by the fact that this stranger could have pinpointed me as some heinous criminal; some malicious killer. I didn't even know how my body could do such a thing. I have never even smooshed an ant with my finger, so how could they even think that it was me? I was getting angrier and angrier, because she was terrorizing me and pushing me to say something or to slip up, but there was nothing to slip up about.

Not to mention, my head was still pounding from being hit, and the non-stop badgering kept making it worse. The Tylenol the officers had given me earlier was barely making a dent in the pain, and the awful lighting and smell of the interrogation room didn't help how I was feeling, either. All I could do was sit there listening to her; all while trying to fight to tell the truth and save what life I had left.

"You came here to LA from Missouri right after you lost your only living relative, your grandmother, correct?" the detective asked.

"Yes," I replied.

"You meet this group of young individuals with money and connections, and you push yourself on them because you want to fit in and be one of them." She started pacing before continuing, "Their life is appealing to you, Julie. It's everything you never had. It's everything you've always wanted it to be. And let's face it, these people are beautiful, they're rich, people know who they are. They're, for a lack of a better term, famous." She paused. "And you want to be famous, Julie, right? That's your life goal, isn't it? So, why wouldn't you have a motive to kill someone? Especially someone who you felt was trying to take your place?"

"What are you talking about? I DIDN'T KILL ANYONE. IT WAS THEM. I SWEAR!" I screamed louder and louder.

"So how well did you know Ms. Kane, Julie?"

"Ms. Kane? I don't know a Ms. Kane. What are you talking about?" I was confused why they were asking me about someone that I didn't even know. Why were they accusing me of something that I didn't even do? Why wouldn't they just believe me? With every breath that I took, my world was falling apart. It just kept crumbling with every word coming out of my mouth.

"Come on Julie, Morgan Kane," she said harshly.

"I don't know anyone named Morgan Kane. I promise," I said pleadingly.

"Of course you do, Julie. Morgan Kane, the daughter of Peter Kane. You're in the industry, you must know who he is."

"The actor?" I asked, shaking my head. "I've never met her. Why are you asking me about her?"

"Because, Julie, she was hanging out with Roxy. *Your* best friend, and you didn't like it. You felt like she was taking your place, but you knew that she had more in common with Roxy than you did. You knew that Roxy was about to dump you as a friend because she had Morgan. You were jealous, Julie. So, you killed her," she said, giving me direct eye contact.

"I didn't kill anyone!" Tears began streaming down my cheeks and my cries were harder than before. I was being accused of killing someone that I had never even met, let alone heard of.

"Julie, stop bullshitting us. We know that you did it. You killed her. We have your prints on the gun," the detective told me.

She was trying to scare me; to intimidate me into telling her information. But I didn't have any. All I had was my story; my truth of what had happened, and no one to back up my alibi. The sick part is that Roxy and Dalton weren't even being questioned. They were the ones who had done this terrible thing to a girl for a reason unbeknownst to me, and *I* was being blamed for it. I was being blamed for *murdering* someone. *Murder. Me.*

"Julie, tell us what you did!" She slammed her hands down on the table.

"I didn't do anything, how many times do I have to tell you?" I pleaded.

Hours went by. And with every one of those hours, there was more badgering and repeating the same things over and over again, with the same conclusions from the detectives; that I was guilty. Within those hours—those endless hours—I started to believe them.

"They almost killed me," I cried. "Why can't you help me?"

"Miss Simon, we have no evidence of that."

"One of their friends, Chad Remington. He raped me and I got pregnant."

"Again Miss Simon, we have no record of that. There's no way to prove it."

"Abortion!" I shot up. "I had an abortion. Surely you can get proof there. I went to a doctor and everything."

"What doctor?"

"I don't remember his name; Roxy took me to him. He was somewhere in LA."

"Well, that doesn't give us much, does it, Miss Simon?"

I was feeling defeated. The detectives were rattling my brain, trying to purge me of nonexistent information.

I wanted to give up so badly. But if I gave up, what would happen to me? I was the only one that could fight for myself.

"My doctor! Dr. Haggerty!" I said with excitement after a long while of being within my own thoughts. "I went to him when I wasn't feeling well, shortly after I was raped. He was the one that concluded that I was pregnant. Contact him and he will tell you that I am not lying. I even told him that I was raped."

"Okay, Miss Simon, but you said that it was shortly after you were raped. Did you get checked out at the hospital right after this rape happened?"

I sunk into my chair. I knew that I should have gone to a hospital right away, but how was I supposed to know that all of *this* would be happening to me now? Everything so far was pointing to me. My fingerprints were on the gun, even though I didn't even see a gun. I was knocked out. That's all that I knew.

"No," I began to cry again.

"So, there's no way that you can prove that you, in fact, were actually raped, Miss Simon?"

"I guess not." More tears. "Wait. There was a note left with roses at the front desk of the hotel that I was raped in. And the girl! The girl at the front desk must have seen the rapist. You can contact her and ask."

I waited alone for two hours in the interrogation room, waiting for the detectives to let me go. As I sat there, I started to think about everything that had happened over the past few months, trying to piece together clues or come up with any information that would prove my innocence. But the more time I spent alone in that tiny room with my own thoughts, the more I started to think that maybe it *was* possible that I had done this unspeakable crime.

What if I had met Morgan Kane and didn't like her? I had no idea what she looked like, but maybe I had blocked her from my memory like I had all of the attacks from Roxy and the guys. It's possible. I *had* been struck in the back of my head. Or what if I just drank too much that night on the beach, and had dreamt that I was drowning and that no one was helping me? The mind can and does play funny tricks on you.

I *had* taken the ecstasy that night at Dalton's before we went out on the strip. What if I was so high that I put the moves on Chad and our sex was consensual? What if the burglary that Chad and Sebastian did at my apartment was just me going crazy and messing everything up in my own home? What if I convinced myself into killing someone because I wanted to be one of them so badly? Because I wanted Dalton so badly that I couldn't let anyone get in my way? So many thoughts kept flooding my mind. So many stupid, stupid and irrational thoughts.

Detective Johnson finally came back into the room, alone.

"Miss Simon, we contacted that hotel and the woman you mentioned at the front desk."

"And?" I asked, pleading for an answer.

"She never saw a man leave your room that night."

"What?" I was so confused. "What about the roses?

Surely, she saw who had given her the roses to give to me."

"They were delivered from a flower shop nearby."

There was silence.

"We contacted them to see who had placed the order and," Detective Johnson paused. "Miss Simon, Morgan Kane was the one that placed the order."

"What?" I was even more confused than before. "How can that be? I don't even know who she is. Like I've told you so many times, I've never met her. I've never even heard her name until you told it to me earlier!" I broke down into a defeated sob. "I didn't do it. Roxy and Dalton are trying to set me up. I'm telling you the truth. Why won't you believe me?" I looked Detective Johnson in the eyes. "What can I do to get you to believe me? This just doesn't make any sense."

No matter how many times I tried to plead my innocence, the detectives were convinced that I was guilty. After another hour of interrogation, detective Johnson stepped out. I was exhausted by that point, and the weight of the blame for something that I didn't do being placed on my shoulders was dragging me down more and more.

I was arrested for the murder of Morgan Kane; the daughter of Peter Kane, and someone that I didn't even know and had never met before.

The trial began, and I had everyone in the world

against me, except for Jeffery and Dawson. Even though I had been so awful to them, they were the only ones that believed me. They were the ones that had warned me all those months ago when I began my friendship with Roxy. It's like they knew. They had warned me to never forget them, but I did. I had been too swooped up in the glow of the high life and decided that they weren't worthy enough for my newfound ego. And because I was too into myself and feeling like I was better than them, I let these disgusting people, these *murderers*, into my life. And ultimately, they framed me for something so horrible. I should have known when they tried to kill me. You would think so, right?

But Jeffrey and Dawson went above and beyond for me. They put their careers on the line by simply being associated with me. I'm sure people turned on them, but no matter what, they were there every day, sitting behind me and silently rooting for the girl I once was, the girl they once knew. And when everything started, without hesitation, they helped me seek a decent legal counsel to go up against the lawyers who were representing the Kane's, who, of course, were the best lawyers in the country for something as high profile as this was. They made sure that my lawyers would fight for me; fight for my innocence.

Jeffrey—my sweet Jeffrey—was even called to take the stand to testify about Roxy handing him a note to give to me. Although that would have been key evidence for my case, Jeffrey hadn't read it and I had thrown it away, so it didn't really matter in the end. When he walked off of the stand he just looked at me somberly and mouthed, "I'm sorry."

The worst day of the trial though was when they called his name. My heart immediately fell to the pit of my stomach. Even in a state of such dismay, he still had me. Somehow, he even seemed more handsome if that was possible. I don't know if it was because he had hurt me again in such an awful way, which seemed to be the pattern of my love for him, or if it was because I hadn't seen him in a while. Since that night. Either way, he still made my heart race. He didn't look at me at all—not once. After everything he and I had shared together, the connection that we had built, the love that I know was there forming, he still didn't have the courage to look me in the eyes. He seemed ashamed and it was because he knew that he was lying. He was protecting her, and I had no idea why.

And then she took the stand. Of course, she looked as beautiful and radiant as the first time I saw her. That confidence and arrogance emitting out of her was already making everyone fall in love with a monster. She was out to get me, and she knew that she would win.

"Miss Harrington, please explain to us, in your own words what happened."

"I don't know any other way to say it other than she was obsessed with me. I mean, I don't really blame her. We come from two very different families. Hers was, well, she didn't really have one." She looked directly at me then. She would look at the jury and then back at me continuously throughout her testimony. "And as you know, my father is a very successful director. She must have seen that as an opportunity for herself." She then started to appear sad, like she was actually hurt over the situation. But I was the only one to see right through her for the conniving, sadistic bitch that she is. "I'm sorry, I just lost my best friend and someone who I thought was my other one." Her fake sobs were conveying enough that I could tell the jury felt for her. It was the performance of a lifetime, really. Far better than any scene I could ever do. The entire courtroom was eating it up; every word, every lie, and every fabrication of the truth. They were hung up on her words. Yet mine, the actual truth, meant nothing.

My team advised me that I shouldn't take the stand because it could harm my case and make me look even more guilty. But I wasn't going to let Roxy win. I couldn't. The only thing that I had to defend myself against her were my words, and those words would do more harm than anything she ever did to me. By the time I did take the stand, I could barely recognize myself. I had lost weight from the stress and looked tired and haggard from not sleeping very much. I was constantly worried about how I was going to get out of this. When I began to speak, it was like the whole world fell silent. They were all waiting for me to give the gruesome details. Every last, little one. I'm sure they were all very disappointed when I maintained my innocence and continued to plead, with whoever was really listening, that it wasn't me.

"You keep saying that, Miss Simon, but all of the

evidence is proving your plea to be false. And you know what happens when you lie to the court, correct?"

Sitting there frustrated and fed up, I kept crying, "I didn't do it. I didn't do it." With every sob that poured out of me was the truth. But they just thought I was acting.

I was found guilty and sentenced to life in prison. But I didn't do it. I didn't kill anyone. It was all a dream.

Chapter Sixteen

"So, what do you think about all of this, Ms. Simon?"

"I mean, I just told you the whole story. What am I supposed to think? But you know, it's kind of funny..."

"What's funny?"

"How no one cared about me until now. I mean, as a little girl I always dreamed of moving to Hollywood and becoming famous, where everybody knew who I was. I just never thought that *this* would be the way that it would happen. You know, as the 'Hollywood Psycho' or whatever it is that they call me. It's funny, because I've been in here for over a year now since I had my mental breakdown, just sitting in a room all alone. Sometimes they've even put my arms in restraints so that I won't 'hurt myself.' And all I do every day is repeat those few months over and over in my head, trying to remember any little detail that would help me. But when you're trapped in a place where people think that you're crazy, you kind of start to believe it too. The mind is funny that way. You start to think that maybe you did this *one* bad thing, and your brain *chose* to block it out, and so you start to believe that you *are* this crazy person. And not just any kind of crazy person, someone that's clinically insane. Someone who was so weak-minded that they would go out and kill someone else because they were manipulated into doing it. I don't just believe that I could be this person anymore, I know that I am."

"I don't think you are."

"Well, that's very kind of you. There's a lot of people out there that would beg to differ."

Silence.

"Do you ever get any visitors?"

"Sometimes Jeffery and Dawson come to see me. They're the only ones that care. I'm an orphan, remember? They try to lift my spirits, but I always tell them to forget about me and move on with their lives. They have full ones ahead of them. I don't want to be a burden to them. But they're the only ones that actually believe me. You know, you should always trust your gut and put that trust in the people that actually care about you. People who *don't* try to kill you or frame you for murder. That's where it's *my* fault. If I would have only listened to my gut, and mostly to them, my life would be completely different right now. Heck, I could actually be a movie star, or be in love. Who knows?"

"Has anyone else tried to visit you? Like, Dalton Blake?"

"Ha! I don't know if I would even let him see me."

"Why?"

"Because look at me. I'm a 'murderer,' and he's one of the two people that put me here. What would he want to see me for?"

"I don't know, maybe to explain things or explain how he feels about you?"

"How he feels about *me*? Oh, I'm sure that he holds me in the highest regard and is absolutely in love with me. I mean, how could he not be? He almost let me drown, he drugged me, betrayed me. Oh! And set me up for murder. He is so in love with me! Come on, please. He is what his reputation is, the bad boy that only cares about himself and gets every girl wrapped around his finger. I'm the perfect example. He gets whatever he wants, whenever he wants. But I will tell you this, I see him in my dreams. And in those dreams, we live in a little house back home in Arrow Rock, and we have a little girl and a little boy. We're happy. We're in love. He sneaks up behind me when I'm doing dishes and holds me, and then gives me little kisses on my neck. I'll spin around and we just stare into each other's eyes, feeling every bit of love that we felt when we were alone together. Those dreams make each day easier. Yeah, he's that type of guy."

"What type of guy?"

"The one that gets in your heart and can never get out. The one that always stays with you, no matter what may have happened, even if they were the ones that wronged you. You'll always love him, and you can't really explain why, you just will. I don't know if everyone gets a love like that, or if it's just something I made up in my head because I'll never get to experience it again. But he's *that* type of guy. He's unforgettable."

Silence.

"Ms. Simon, have you read or watched the news lately?"

"Why should I? People like me *are* the news. I don't want to see that."

"So, no one has told you that your friend Roxanne Harr..."

"I wouldn't exactly call her my friend."

"So, no one has told you that she has committed suicide?"

"I probably should have done that. Funny, huh?"

"How so?"

"Well, she had everything imaginable in life and she took the easy way out. God, it's just like her, always being selfish."

"Ms. Simon..."

"Please, just call me Jules."

"Okay. Jules. They're reopening your case."

"Why?"

"Because Roxy left a note before she took her own life."

"Okay, so?"

"It said, 'Tell Jules I'm sorry.'"

"And what's that supposed to mean?"

"Jules, Roxanne Harrington confessed that she was behind it all, and that it was her and Dalton Blake that were the ones that killed Morgan Kane. Not you."

Silence.

"What do you think about that?" the reporter asked.

"That I wish I was one of them."

"One of who?"

"My palm trees."

Roxy's Note

There was something I'd always wanted to do in life, something that fascinated me in an intoxicating kind of way. It's something that I now realize only very few people actually commit to doing, and that was killing someone. It's not that I have this inkling to just want to go out and commit a ton of murders, I've just always been curious as to what it would feel like. You know, kind of like when you see someone riding a bike on the street and you wonder what it would be like to just turn the steering wheel a little bit and clip them. Maybe that's just me. It's not something that I ever thought I would do until I found myself in a position where someone pissed me off so badly that it seemed like the best idea. The only idea.

I didn't have many friends growing up and I always found myself getting along better with guys than I did girls. But when I was a teenager, I met Morgan Kane in a class we shared together at our private school. I took a liking to her. She was smart and studious, kind of a goodie

goodie. Let's just say when we were out partying she would never partake. She wasn't the type of person that I would tell all of my secrets to, but she was someone that I chose to let be around me.

The years passed and we were friendly. We hung out a lot but she was starting to bore me. Even though her father was a successful actor, she still wanted to pursue college and make something of herself. She could have lived off of her father like the rest of us, but she said that it didn't feel right. I didn't quite understand how you would want to pursue hard work when you could be handed, and had been handed, everything for your entire life. We got into an argument once at a party where I had done a little too much coke. She told me that I had a problem and that I needed help. I got really angry with her and decided to slip her a roofie just for the fun of it. Well, she didn't like that and in turn went to my father and told him about my "problem." My father told me that I had to go to rehab or I would get cut off. I begrudgingly went to rehab for a month. When I came back, I pretended to be the world's best daughter. I kept thanking him for saving my life and setting me up on the right path. Thankfully I had Chad and Sebastian to help me score once I got home. I didn't do as much because I needed my father to keep footing my bills. When Morgan found out that I was using again, she went back to my father and told him. That's when daddy cut me off and I was even more pissed than before.

I'm not the type to sit around and let people walk all over me. I'm the one very much on the side of retaliation, even though my outward demeanor may convey a different message. I've always been told that I'm beautiful, and I know that. I take great pride in myself and how I act because I am at a *far* better advantage than most people. I come from a family of status and I know how to work the system.

When my father cut me off and kicked me out to "teach me a lesson," I knew that I had to get rid of Morgan. The only way to do that would be to do that one thing that always fascinated me. I had to kill her. I don't know when, but somewhere along the way I had mentioned to Dalton what I wanted to do. He said that he'd wondered what that would feel like too. He said that although he would never do it, and couldn't understand how someone could, he had thought about it before. I asked him if he wanted to be a part of my little plan. He reluctantly agreed. Well, he agreed because I told him that if he didn't help me that I would casually mention to the press his father's multiple malpractice cases that he covered up. Dr. Blake had too big of an ego to let anything ruin his career. But when the same thing happens to multiple women, one of which being my mother, it's fishy how none of it, not even one, gets out. The only way I knew about any of it was because I saw my mother fall ill and heard my Father screaming into the phone about how he was going to "sue that motherfucker." Even though Dalton had some major mommy issues and would say that he hated his Father, he still respected him, although I think that it was a fear-driven respect. Dr. Blake was always hard on Dalton. He bullied him around, always telling him that he didn't have any motivation or determination in life. He would say that Dalton would never amount to anything. But in public, he couldn't be more proud of having *the* Dalton Blake as his son. Being the son that he was, Dalton didn't want to do anything that would ever hurt his father's reputation, or the family name. So when I told him that I would let that little secret of mine slip, he knew that he couldn't say no to me.

I didn't know how I was going to do it, though. I needed it to be flawless and have no trace leading back to me, whatsoever. Basically, I needed to either do it some- where no one would ever find the body or have someone else take the fall. But it had to be me, the one to actually do it. I needed to feel what it felt like.

Then on that fateful day when I went to try to see my father about giving me some money, or at least letting me come home, I met the perfect opportunity. I don't believe in coincidences. I think things happen how they're meant to happen. And when I had just been rejected by my father, yet again in my life, I saw this young, naïve girl losing it over the rejection from him as well. I knew she would be the perfect person to execute my plan. I had built up a wall against my father. I knew how to be on his good side and how to get on his bad, intentionally. This time I was unintentionally there and wanted to be back where I knew that I belonged. My father is a hard man to please, and when you haven't done that, the wrath that he can put upon you is not for the faint of heart. That's how I knew Julie Simon would be the perfect pawn in the game that I was about to play.

Immediately I went up to her, introduced myself and invited her to lunch. She was striking in a nonconventional way. Very plain. Ordinary. You could tell she was normal. She was definitely not from around here, which made it even easier to get her to be my friend. She wanted my life, the way I lived, the way I looked. But my life was only ever something she could ever dream about. Chad, Sebastian and Dalton were at the diner when we walked in, and I gave a look to Dalton to let him know that our plan was in motion.

We had talked about different scenarios before. He knew that if we did find someone to frame, it would be a girl. He would act as if he was interested and make it seem as though he were falling in love with her. Dalton had always been the envy of every girl's affection and he knew it. He played into it. That's how he got every girl he's ever been with, even me in a way. He wasn't actually as dark and brooding as he appeared to be. He's soft under that hard exterior, but definitely has a way of charming everyone he meets. Like I predicted, she fell in love with him as soon as they met. It was almost too easy.

I remember thinking, after I dropped her off, that I hadn't actually enjoyed another girl's company since I first met Morgan all of those years ago. That's when I decided to pick up the pace in my little game. I invited her over for a girl's night. Jules was awestruck about me, about everything I have. Who wouldn't be? I could tell that she was trying to keep her chin off of the floor when I was giving her a tour of my house. But all in all, I enjoyed her being there. I was actually very lucky that my parents weren't there that night. They were attending a benefit after the auditions and staying at a hotel. Our housekeeper was the one to tip me off about that. She always loved me and hated how my parents treated me. She was the only constant in my life.

I made it a point to tell Jules that Dalton liked her because I had to keep her wanting more of him. She needed to want more of us. Have you ever had one of those moments where a genius idea randomly flashes in your head and you think, *wow, this is brilliant?* Well, that happened while she was over. I told her that I wanted her to be a part of our group and in turn she accepted. I had an even better plan brewing, though. I didn't want to just use her as my scapegoat. I wanted to have some more fun with her. I mean, if I was already going to be doing this, I might as well go all out and put her through some shit first.

Chad and Sebastian liked my idea about an initiation, but Dalton didn't. Before I go on, I should tell you that Chad and Sebastian had no idea what the true intentions were. They wouldn't have gone along with it and they would have given everything away before the deed was done. They're always too high to fully trust and too pretty for prison.

Dalton seemed like he was disinterested in my plan to drug her and put her in the ocean at night to see what would happen. That's another one of those things you kind of wonder about. What would happen in that kind of scenario? And now I had the means to find out. I remember him saying, "Why do you have to torture the poor girl, Roxy? She seems really nice. We're already framing her for something much bigger. Why do you have to go and make it more than what it should be?"

"Because it's murder, Dalton. Remember? That's huge! And this is our only opportunity to do it and not get caught. So, why not have a little more fun and see what else we can get away with?" I said back to him.

"You're crazy, Roxy. I'm not gonna have any part of that. I'll be there, of course, but just to make sure that she's okay."

I knew that he liked her, and it made me kind of mad. He never liked anyone, like truly liked them. He would just fuck 'em and leave them. That's the part that I didn't see coming in any of this. That he would actually fall in love with her. He didn't admit it to my face at first, but I knew that he did and I could see it happening right before my eyes. I think I brushed it off because I was more interested in seeing out the end goal than focusing on Dalton's feelings. Those didn't matter to me. My sights were set on what I wanted to do, and only on that.

He was the one that saved her. I tried making out with him because I had just snorted a line and was feeling good. I grabbed him but he pushed me off and ran into the water.

The following day I went to her place to check up on her. I may have felt a little bad seeing as how Chad, Sebastian and I weren't doing anything. We just watched. When I got there, she looked terrible. She started to tell me about a dream that she had. I laughed because it was funny. I also got to see the look on her face when I told her that that wasn't a dream at all. It had actually happened. I did, however, say that I didn't make out with Dalton because I didn't want her to not trust me. Having her trust me was a key component to my game. So, to get her thinking about something else, I told her that I had never had a friend like her before. That she was more than a best friend. I left her happy.

A few days later, Dalton took her out on a date. He tried to play it off as if he didn't want to take her. He wasn't good about hiding his true feelings. I told him all of the places to take her because I knew that she would think he was so romantic showing her places that really reflect what it means to live in our world. I told him to charm her and leave her wanting more. I told him to do whatever it took except kiss her or sleep with her. Imagine the surprise on my end when I found out that he had actually kissed the bitch. That right there made me realize that he wasn't all that trustworthy, and I had to think of something else to continue to make him loyal to me.

My boiling point with him, though, was the night we were going to The Viper Room. I saw the way he was looking at her, the way he was longing for her. It was like he couldn't wait for them to be alone together. When we were heading out to the car, I hid on the other side of the wall when he pulled her back and I saw him kiss her. I've told you before, I'm a retaliation type of person, so that's what I did. When we got to the club, I slipped Chad a room key and whispered, "You know what to do." It was something I had casually mentioned to him the night before just in case something wasn't going my way. He seemed all too eager about the opportunity. He liked being a girl's first. He liked to brag to us when he would get a virgin. Those poor girls, too drunk to even know what they were doing. We did get a kick out of his stories, though. After he left her, he headed to her apartment with Sebastian where they made it look like someone had broken in. I was already so deep into this that it was hard to not fulfill every thought of torment I could throw at her.

When Dalton found out about Chad raping her, oh he was pissed. Rightfully so, I guess. But I had never seen him that angry. He walked into the room and sucker punched Chad in the face. Then he started to yell at me and kicked me out. Thankfully my parents were out of town shooting my father's movie, so I was able to be home for a little while without any disturbances. That is, until she called me a few short hours later and told me what had happened. I played my part of the best friend so well and had her come over ASAP to get to the bottom of it. I had her stay with me for a few days, which was actually kind of nice. It almost felt like she was the sister I never had. I mean, being an only child has a lot of perks, but it would have been nice, and a little less lonely, if I had someone to scheme with.

The night that everything changed was the night she came to thank Dalton for having her apartment cleaned up. That was definitely where I slipped up, and I own up to my faults. Dalton was mad at me and not talking to me, but I went back to his house when my parents came home for a few days. He told me to leave, that he didn't want to talk to me anymore. I reminded him about our plan and about what we were trying to do. I reminded him that I could pin it on him just as easily as I could pin it on her. When I feel like I'm on top of the world, like my power rules over everyone, that's when I need to have sex the most. It makes me feel alive. I came on to Dalton. I always had to be the one to come on to him. We've slept together a few times before, but this time was different. I had to force him to have sex with me. But once he got going, he was into it. Then she appeared and Dalton turned into a weak puppy. I remember kind of shrugging her presence off but thinking, *Great, what am I going to do now?* Not him. He went to chase after her.

When Dalton got back to the room, he seemed frustrated. I knew what was wrong, but I had to ask anyway. "What's wrong?"

"God, Roxy, you fucking know."

"No, I don't think I do. What's wrong?"

"Roxy, I don't think we should do this anymore. It's not worth it. We don't even talk to Morgan anymore and she's a sweet girl, Roxy. And I..."

"You what?" I asked, hoping he wasn't going to say what I thought he was going to say.

"Just stop messing with her, okay?"

"Okay, fine. I'll think of something else. Would that be okay with you?" He looked at me, shaking his head before walking out of the room. But leaving her alone would be too easy and not as fun. I decided that I just wouldn't tell him when I did anything to her. Besides, I had Chad and Sebastian that could help me without knowing what they were doing. I told them that she and I were having a little bit of a tiff and that I wanted them to keep calling her to hang out with us. They obviously obliged and did what I told them. When she wouldn't return any of my calls or messages, I decided that I had to take a different approach. I showed up at her job to put the pressure on, but she couldn't face me and ran away. I asked for a pen and wrote her a note. "You know you're still one of us." I left it with some really hot guy to give to her. But there was still no way of getting her to come around. I knew that I, personally, had messed up my chance at committing the perfect crime. But if you know me, or have been reading this, then you know I'm not someone that easily quits. If she was going to ignore me, then I would make myself impossible to ignore.

I showed up at her apartment and sat outside her door, waiting for her to come home one day. She didn't have any other friends so it wasn't like she would be out all day, she was bound to come back. I waited for about an hour before she showed up, looking like she was in a daze, like she had seen a ghost. She tried to push me out of the way but ended up falling to the ground in tears. I don't like seeing people cry, which isn't something that I'm forthcoming to admit because it shows a side of weakness. But something made me bend down to comfort her. That's when she told me that she was pregnant. I remember being in actual shock. I knew that Chad liked virgins, but I thought he would at least be a little bit smarter about it. Now, I love Chad. He's one of the best people I know, but having one of him around is enough. I told her that I would help her get it taken care of, so I did.

When I got back to Dalton's, I walked in in a fit of rage. "You fucking asshole."

Chad sat there slouched in a chair with a joint in his hand looking around. "Who me? What did I do?"

"You fucking got her pregnant."

"Oh, shit." Sebastian sat up.

"You didn't use a fucking condom?"

"What? It was her first time. That never happens."

"Yes, it does, asshole. I'm taking her to get an abortion tomorrow."

"Oh, come on Roxy, let her keep it. I want to see a little Chad running around this place," Sebastian laughed.

I glared at the both of them, "You dumb shits better not tell Dalton. Do you fucking understand me?"

"Why would he care?" Sebastian continued laughing.

"Just don't fucking tell him."

They shook their heads and went back to smoking, Sebastian laughing at Chad, calling him dad. That was an unexpected turn of events that I didn't want to have to deal with.

When I took her to the appointment, I can honestly say I felt bad. I admit it. I actually think I'm starting to admit a lot of things now. Once everything was taken care of, I regained my focus on what the original plan was: to kill Morgan Kane. My focus was now shifted back to that.

I needed Jules to trust me again. I needed her to feel like I wasn't going to do anything to hurt her. So, I invited her over to Dalton's a few nights later to hang out and get a feel on where her headspace was. It wasn't in a good spot. I really hate when I'm put in a position where I feel like I'm being used to get to my father, and that's where she put me. I tried to tell myself to ignore her, to not pay attention to what she asked. But when she snapped, that was my last straw. I couldn't hold it in any longer, everything that I'd wanted to say to her since we first met. Everything was dragged out and all about her, whining about this or that. Listening to her stories and pretending to be interested in her naïve perception on life was too much for me to bear anymore. I know firsthand that if no one is there to help you, the only person that you can rely on is yourself. I had relied on myself my entire life to get the things that I wanted from my parents. Remember, you're the only true person you can trust after all.

When I knew I was going to commit to killing Morgan, I had to change my mindset to something I had never experienced. Not only would I have to rely on myself for executing my plan, I would have to rely on the naivety of someone who needed others to help her through life. When someone needs someone else that badly, their biggest fault is their weakness, and it shows. Jules was weak. She needed guidance more than anyone I had ever met. She didn't know how to stand up for herself and when she finally got the courage to try, she proved me right into knowing that she was the right person for me to pin the murder on. Chad and Sebastian walked in at the perfect moment. They had no idea what was going on but they somehow came in clutch and helped me get out what I needed to say to her. The look of shock on her face when she found out that Chad was the one that raped her was worth everything that we had done to her. She looked terrified. She looked helpless. She looked alone. That's when I knew, no one was going to miss her. She only had herself and she didn't know how to use that.

As soon as she ran out of Dalton's, I told him that it was happening that night. His eyes widened as he pleaded with me to not go through with it. He told me not to blame Julie. He kept calling her Julie, like she was more than the pawn I had created her to be. It was like she meant something to him, something more than I would ever be to him. That's when he finally broke and said that he loved her and that he wouldn't let me do it. He was going to try and stop me. That's the funny thing about a weak man, their weaknesses get blindsided by their truths. And his was that he was in love with the wrong person.

When she hung up on me, I handed the phone to him. When he tried to push it away, I forced it on him. She came, just like I knew she would. I had to make it seem like it was all an accident, like something went wrong. Dalton was fine because he was beside himself. He was pacing and mumbling, very out of character for him, but it worked out beautifully in that moment. Obviously, Jules immediately walked up to him. But it gave me the perfect opportunity to grab the gun and hit her in the back of the head. She fell straight to the ground. I felt calm and at ease as I wiped the gun down, getting any of my DNA off. Then I proceeded to put her prints on the handle before throwing it in the brush nearby. Every move was thought about numerous times and in different ways. There was no room for error, but I could only account for myself.

Dalton was in shock. He could barely move. When I told him to get in the car, he fell to his knees next to her, crying. He kept telling her over and over how sorry he was and how much he loved her. He said that he wanted to be with her and he tried to stop me. He was talking as if he were a different person, not the Dalton Blake that I knew and grew up with. Not the Dalton Blake that wasn't fazed by anything, where things just came easy to him. Not the Dalton Blake I was in love with. He seemed changed, he seemed unrecognizable. It was like she had made an impact on him and I knew that he would never be the same. I mean, who would be after killing someone?

We didn't talk the entire drive home to his house. We didn't talk when I packed up my things and moved back home. We didn't talk for a while after everything happened. We didn't even talk when we saw each other at the trial. He didn't look at me the same and I couldn't look at him the same either. He was actually in love with someone else.

I fell back into using, harder, but I had a better way of covering it up. I had to keep my parents off my back but needed the cash flowing in to fund my little habit. I had convinced them that I was clean and that I missed being with them, so they let me come back home. It was easy to avoid them because they never wanted to be around me. That is, until the trial where we had to put up a united front to protect my father's image. Those were some of the most miserable days, trying to stay clean when all I wanted to do was drown everything out. I honestly don't even really remember what I said on the stand because immediately after I got off, I went straight to the bathroom and snorted away any sorrows I had. Chad and Sebastian started to hang out at my place. They said that Dalton kicked them out, that he was shut off and they didn't know why. They talked about Jules and how crazy it was that someone so sweet and innocent could do something so insanely harsh, especially to someone as nice as Morgan. They said they didn't even know that the two of them had ever met one another. It's because they hadn't. I always sat in silence because I feel like silence can sometimes be more powerful than words. I let them ramble on and on, never giving away what I actually knew to be the truth. They were sitting right next to a murderer. *The murderer.* They were sharing joints with one, even the occasional roll in the sack. It was me. I was the murderer. The murderer of not one, not two, but three people. One physically and two psychologically.

Here is where I now find myself. I'm in a little bit of a mess, I guess, because I don't think that I actually ever quite enjoyed my life. It's been full of pain and lack of acceptance from my parents, which is probably why I felt the way that I did towards wanting to kill someone. Although, I never saw myself as being this kind of person. I guess we all could be in some strange way, we're human after all. We're a creature that kills for food. We kill in defense of oneself. We kill to protect others. If we were in the wild, it would all be okay, but since society has deemed it unacceptable and wrong, that makes me unacceptable and that's something I don't want to be. I'm perfect, I always have been. So I can be a little bit of a bitch, but who isn't? But there's this lingering notion that I am now *not* perfect, and it won't go away. It consumes my every thought and makes me not want to be here anymore. Like the one thing that I'd always wanted to do, that fascinated me, was something I should have just done to myself. I don't want to have to think about it anymore. I don't want to have to think about him, think about her, or the image of me actually pulling the trigger. I want it to all go away.

Anyways, to end this long winded rant, I confess that I was the one to actually murder Morgan Kane. I want to say two final things. The first is to Dalton. You and I will forever be linked, in this lifetime and the next. We won't know when and we won't know how. But our souls are connected and will always find each other no matter where we are, who we're with or what we're doing. Lastly, which may come as a surprise because I've come to realize that I'm a fairly heartless person, but...

...tell Jules I'm sorry.

The End

Acknowledgements

First, I'd like to thank my husband for always believing in me and endlessly supporting this crazy little book dream of mine. Thank you for always questioning "Who the bleep did I marry?" whenever I tell you a new story idea I have. Hopefully one day you'll actually read one of my books!

A huge thank you is to my sweet babies. Because of you two, Mommy really dove deep into finishing this debut novella. I want to show you both that no matter what, your dreams *can* and *will* come true if you go after them. I hope that Mommy has made you proud. And an enormous thank you for taking naps so Mommy could work.

Thank you Mom for always rooting for me. Thank you for reading, and loving, the very early version of this story. You made me want to keep going even though I knew you would like anything I showed you because I'm your daughter. Thank you for the love that you have given me and for showing me that I can do it.

Emi Janisch, a big thank you to you and that little TikTok video you posted about wanting to edit and help indie authors out. I couldn't be more grateful and appreciative of you. You reignited my passion for this story and really helped me get it to completion. I will forever be grateful for you. I look forward to working with you on future stories. And I hope to one day hug you in person.

To my betas, without you and your encouragement, Hollywood Psycho: The Julie Simon Story wouldn't be in readers' hands today. Thank you so much for taking the time to help an aspiring author pursue her dreams and for loving this story as much as I do.

To the script writing college professor that I can't remember his name. Thank you for assigning a film treatment as our semester final because that's how I came up with the idea for this story. And years later when it still wouldn't leave my head, I decided to give my characters a voice and put them into the words that are in this book. Without this class, my dream would not have been realized, so I thank you sir.

Lastly, a huge thank you to you, the reader, for taking a chance on a little indie author who had a story to tell. Without you, my dream wouldn't be complete.

If you could review it on Amazon, Goodreads, Barnes and Noble etc., I would be so grateful and appreciate you even more. Stay tuned for the next one!

Website: brittrothauthor.com

About the Author

Brittany lives in Southern California with her husband, two children and three dogs. She likes to think of her life as a rom-com, set in a comedy club, with occasional musical numbers that don't quite get the rave reviews she hopes for. However, the critics are three and four-years-old, so she lets it slide. But her life is full of love, fun and laughs as each moment is inspiration that fuels her imagination to keep telling stories.